Margaux with an X

Margaux with an X

RON KOERTGE

CANDLEWICK PRESS
CAMBRIDGE, MASSACHUSETTS

First edition 2004

Portions of this novel previously appeared in "Brutal Interlude," a short story first published in *Destination Unexpected*, edited by Donald R. Gallo.

Extract from "Black Fairy Tale" by Elizabeth Spires courtesy of the author.

Library of Congress Cataloging-in-Publication Data

Koertge, Ronald.
Margaux with an X / Ron Koertge. — 1st ed.
p. cm.
Summary: Margaux, known as a "tough chick" at her Los Angeles high school, makes a connection with Danny, who, like her, struggles with the emotional impact of family violence and abuse.
ISBN 0-7636-2401-2
[1. Emotional problems — Fiction. 2. Sexual abuse victims — Fiction. 3. Family violence — Fiction. 4. Los Angeles (Calif.) — Fiction.] I. Title.
PZ7.K81825Mar 2004
[Fic] — dc22 2003065279

2 4 6 8 10 9 7 5 3

Printed in the United States of America

This book was typeset in Giovanni Book.

Candlewick Press
2067 Massachusetts Avenue
Cambridge, Massachusetts 02140

visit us at www.candlewick.com

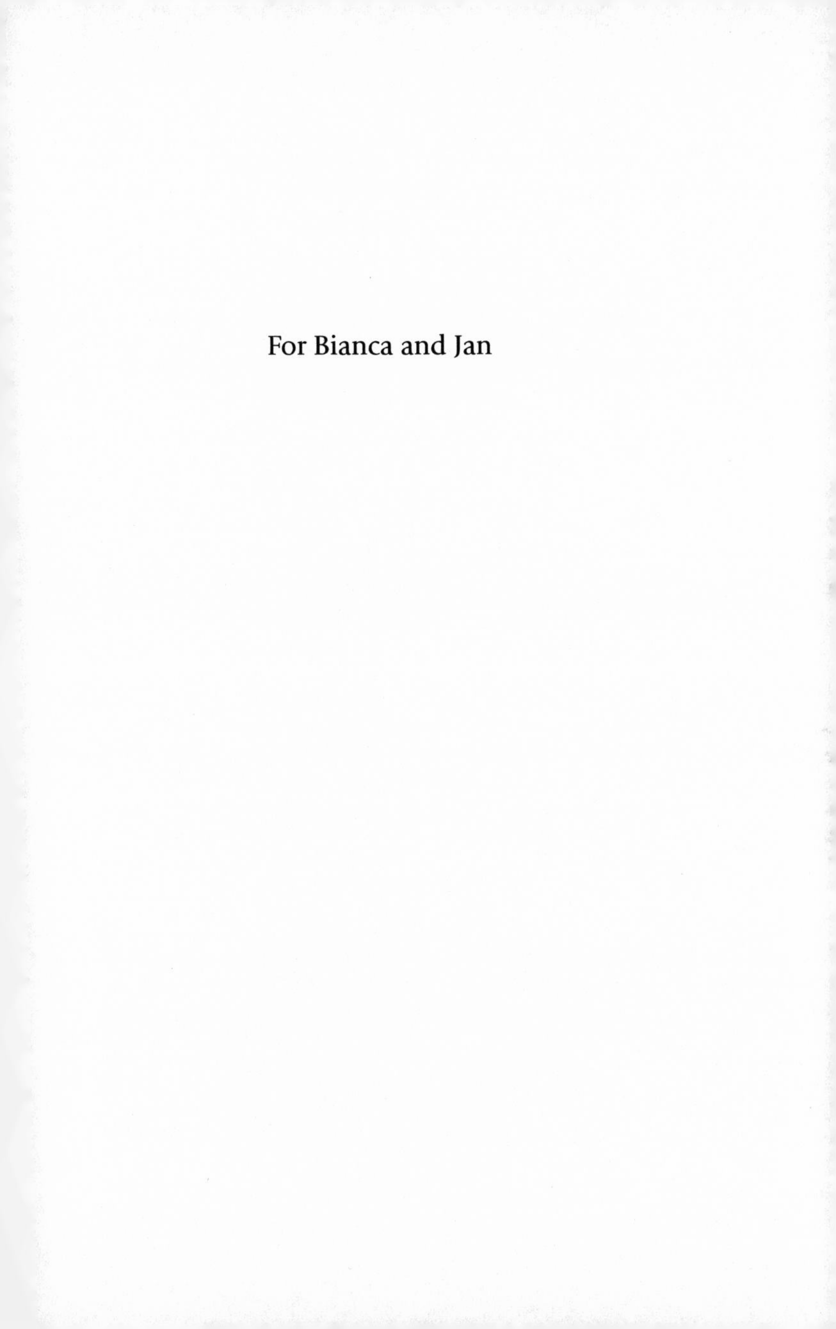

For Bianca and Jan

ANYTHING

to get out of that apartment. Away from her mother, the two TVs, the Home Shopping Network. Margaux abandons homework, heads for bustling, smog-shrouded, gridlocked Arcadia, which is somehow named after a pastoral region of ancient Greece.

She wants to be around people; she wants to be alone. Sara's not answering the phone: that's bad. Or good. Or both.

The drive is okay: A.C. on high (it's torrid in Los Angeles, with the usual muslin-yellow sky), radio up, some gratifying amiable/envious/admiring/

lubricious glances. At the mall, she has to park at the top of a new structure, following a ramp so circuitous it's like an inner ear. Is she going to emerge under the invisible stars on Level 5, blue level, or get lost inside some enormous aural labyrinth? Who would ever find her if she did?

Not her mother—*Honey, you know I hate to drive.*

Not her father—*Can this wait? The third race is about to go off.*

Not Sara—*Call me back, okay? I'm talking to Brad.*

She's no more than locked the Mustang when a girl darts out from behind an SUV. The darting, much less the spectrally thin girl on this corporate darkling plain stacked five stories high, gives Margaux the willies. It seems like an inkling of something. A big inkling if that's possible. But an inkling of what?

"It's not smart for a single gal to be alone in an elevator. Let's ride down together," says the wraith in pants that are probably size one string bean. And strappy little shoes, also white. A white top.

Tight. Very tight. So she's all wrapped up. A sexy little mummy.

Inside, "Raindrops Keep Falling on My Head." Margaux's new friend goes to the farthest corner. Instinctively Margaux stands in front of her. She likes this — protecting somebody, taking care. She could do it for a living: Guardian. Champion. Duenna of the Parking Structure. Maybe wear a mask and cape. And when she got old, join a Wiccan coven and bay at the moon.

She tries a little of her specialty — conversation meant to baffle: "Don't you think it's odd that it's crowded in Arcadia? I mean, from what? Too many shepherds?"

The starveling regards her suspiciously. "Which high school do you go to?"

"It's my last year at King. Why?"

"People from King are always weird."

The elevator doors open on a burnished world. Lustrous counters, dazzling displays, the very floor transplendent. Air is greenhouse damp with samples from the purveyors of Dior, all of them pale as Dracula's perpetual fiancées.

Margaux leads the way out of the elevator. Their elevator.

"You're okay now," she says. "Look: people everywhere."

"Thanks. Thanks a lot. I didn't mean what I said about you guys."

"We weird Kings?"

"Sorry. Really."

Margaux watches her go. She (whoever she is) hasn't got a purse or a wallet. She doesn't want to buy anything. She just wants to be in the store. Wants to pause empty-handed by a cardboard promo for this month's fragrant rage: Dark Stranger. Which shows a coarse but sensitive, roughly tender atheist, one gloved hand beside the throttle. For fourteen bucks, a villain in a bottle. Those guys. Sara's type. And hers sometimes, because Sara said so.

Margaux considers her shopping options: no way is she trying on clothes, because that means walking into the maze of cubicles where some woman behind a half-drawn curtain stares into a three-way mirror and weeps because her flesh seems to be melting.

And she doesn't feel like stealing or doing that other thing she and Sara sometimes do, which is—

Up rushes a zealous salesperson. "Are you finding everything you need?"

Ah, if only that were possible. To find everything she needs. But what is that exactly? And if she knew what it was, could she find it in a mall?

Margaux moves a few hangers around, holds up a thing or two, and scowls. Whatever she left home for, it isn't another blouse. She settles for the exit.

This time she shares the elevator with two couples. The husbands gaze at Margaux; the wives glare at the husbands. She turns to the girls, not two years older than she.

"Is there anyplace else to shop?" she asks. "This place stinks."

The wives glance at each other. They shake their heads together, as if they'd practiced.

"I'm not from here." Even a little lie makes Margaux feel better.

One of the girls wears shoes that look like fungus. "This is a really good mall," she says defensively.

The door opens with a ping. The husbands wait for Margaux. One leans over to hold the door. Then lets it close on his wife.

Margaux doesn't turn around but hears packages tumble, and out spills jealousy, rancor, and suspicion. Sara would laugh; Margaux just walks faster.

Parked right beside her is a man already asleep in his Saturn, a man almost surely waiting for his wife. A copy of the *Daily Racing Form* lies open across his chest. It rises and falls as he breathes. Connected by tunnels and paths, this mall is maybe a mile from Santa Anita Racetrack, a place Margaux hasn't been since she was ten. And the last place she wants to go.

Fifteen minutes later, she bumps through the turnstile, victim of some gruesome undertow. And automatically buys a racing program. She always bought the program when she came with her dad.

The seller knew her, would lean over and take the dollar. "Good luck, sweetie."

"Hey! Wait up."

It's a guy. Carrying a camera with a long, dark, inquisitive snout. And sporting a letterman's jacket. The enormous *B* (Go, Broncos!) festooned with memorabilia: a tiny winged foot, tennis racket from Lilliput, a silver heart, but more a *milagro* than a Valentine's keepsake. Oh, yes, and he also wears the air of a deposed prince.

"Just a wild guess," says Margaux, "but do you go to Bethel?"

"Graduated last June. I'm working at Circuit City, but I really want to be a photographer."

He's had lunch at Subway or a similar vendor that fits his budget, and his breath is so earthy and damp, it seems to forecast a monsoon. He runs after her like a dog that can't resist a red carriage with gold spokes.

"You seem to know your way around here," he pants. "Would you answer just one question?"

She feels the salesman's stratagem. He's read a book or listened to a tape: *Would you answer one question, folks? Do you want to save some money today?*

He fondles his Nikon, so Margaux warns him, "Well, don't point that thing at me."

"Ah, c'mon. All pretty girls like to have their picture taken."

"Well, not this pretty girl. And I'm not kidding."

Just then they're brought up short by the winner of the third race being led toward the backstretch by a stable hand. Two or three riders, their silks unbuttoned to reveal heavy, protective vests, sign programs for fans, then hustle toward the jocks' room. One of them, handsome in a tango dancer way, looks directly at Margaux. Who turns away his insolence with a Gorgon's stare.

"I was all-state volleyball," says her companion. He's chatting her up, emphasizing his height and agility, establishing his credentials, his general worthiness. But she hears the wistfulness, too, for the legend he was. Then he rallies.

"I'm supposed to meet some friends. A buddy of mine knows this Mexican kid whose cousin works here. He says a horse named Big Max can't lose."

Margaux nods. "I've heard that one before."

"It doesn't work like that?"

"I don't know. Probably. Sometimes."

The sun is right in her eyes, so he steps in front of her, blocking it, ingratiating himself. All the right moves.

She looks at him more closely: Sara would approve. Dark, straight hair, green eyes, old-fashioned vicar's glasses = cute. But with a vertical line just above the bridge of his nose signifying the beginning of worry. The future, his job, the economy, Saturday night. A lifetime of Saturday nights. It all makes his brow contract.

He puts one hand on her arm. "Want a Coke or something?"

She glances at the gnawed-looking cuticles, the ring on his thumb. "And then what?" she asks. "The phone number, the nervous first date, an early-bird dinner complete with coupon, those tentative kisses, your hopes and dreams? And after that — are you going to pay your roommate to be out so we can have your squalid apartment to ourselves, or maybe I should just climb in your bedroom window once your parents are asleep."

He backs away, palms up. "Whoa. Take it easy. Forget I said anything."

The lines at the betting windows are the same, same lights on the odds board, and all around the same grumbly white noise. There are the topiary horses, the fountain where she used to like to sit on days when the crowd was light. B.T. Before Tony.

This is hard for her. Harder than she thought it was going to be. She's lightheaded.

Inside the snack bar, she loads a little cardboard tray. The cashier glances at her, punches numbers, glances again.

"Did you used to come here a long time ago? With your dad, maybe? You liked the frozen malts, right?"

"My God." She looks at the woman's nametag. It's Mabel. Ageless Mabel.

"Honey, how are you?"

"Barely ambulatory."

"How's your dad?"

That's what she really wants to know. "He's dead."

Out comes her hand. Bejeweled. "Oh, sweetie. He was so handsome. And I just saw him last week."

"It was his heart. He didn't have one."

After an odd look, Mabel cancels everything on her register and gives her the food. *In memoriam.*

Out the door she goes, feeling a little better, a little less burdened: falsehood as restorative.

She peeks at the odds board. Hears the announcer bark, "They're at the post!" Down with the food, out with the program. A glance at the ladder of names. Number seven is Irreconcilable. There's almost nobody in line to bet now. Why not?

Walking away from the window, she's nearly alone. The action is in the other direction—past the betting windows, the beer stands, the double doors to the huge, groomed oval. Down by the paddock, where she's headed, there's nobody except a few girlfriends or wives reading.

Margaux slows down, listens to the call of the race. The crowd gets into it when the horses turn for home, that big wave of longing. Then it's over. A few women squeal. The real players grin or turn the page.

She sits down on a seaweed-green bench. Along he comes. The guy from before.

"We got off on the wrong foot. I wasn't coming on to you. Honest. It really is my first time here." He points. "I really am meeting some friends."

"So meet them." She takes a bite of hamburger, knows she can't finish it.

He glances down at her ticket. "Did you win?"

"Yes."

"How much."

"A hundred or so."

"Wow. How'd you do that?"

Her scorn is hot as a meteor. "Don't act stupid."

"I just want to come out a little ahead. Buy some CDs after."

"A likely story."

"Why all the attitude?"

"Why not?"

Foiled but not defeated, he points to a tunnel. "What's down there?"

"That rather Dante-esque opening leads to the Keg Room."

"Yeah? What goes on in the Keg Room? Oh, by the way"—out comes his hand—"my name's—"

Margaux shakes her head vigorously. "Just listen: down there very pale people watch everything on closed-circuit TV. They eat strange food they bring themselves. If somebody buys a beer and leaves it to go bet, when he gets back, the beer is gone and the plastic cup has a bite out of it. And you didn't ask, but upstairs is the Turf Club: guy in a tuxedo with his hand out. Coats and ties. Everybody smells good." She takes a breath. "In between lie the rest of us. Oh, yeah, and let's not forget Mexico." She points toward the barns. "Hot walkers and grooms. Knife fights on Saturday night. Every *corazón* a broken one."

She grins, pleased with herself. That was a nice little riff.

He, whoever he is, cocks his head. "You go to King, don't you? Your name is Margaux Wilcox."

Just then an outrider leads the field into the walking ring. Margaux stands up, heads that way. She knows what's coming next. Or pretty soon. *You're beautiful.*

"You're—"

She holds up a warning finger. "Don't say it."

"Don't worry; and I'm not gonna take your picture."

"You better go find your friends."

He points to the passing horses. "Tell me about these guys first."

"Girls. Fillies. Two years old. Most of them have never run before. So they're not hurt yet. They haven't been passed along half a dozen times to half a dozen different trainers, one just a little more desperate to win than the next. They actually want to run. They're unspoiled. They break my heart." She turns to him. "Know what they call a thoroughbred who's never won? A maiden. Very Elizabethan, don't you think?"

"And after they win what do they call them?"

"No sleazy metaphors, okay? You're on thin ice as it is. Now shut up so I can scope out these horses."

The first filly is all lathered up, sweat dripping off her belly. Right behind her is a big chestnut with a blaze on her face. Her coat is good, but she's built to go long and this race is short.

"What exactly are you looking for?" He is right beside her, close. Too close.

If they just wouldn't do that. If they just wouldn't do everything they do.

"Inspiration."

The number five horse has a nice way about her, but her name on the program is Happy Banana — too stupid for words.

Then Margaux sees number nine: ears pricked, curious but composed. She watches her walk away. There's not a drop of kidney sweat. She points to her name — Brutal Interlude — and he, Mr. Pronoun, grins.

They wander toward the windows with everybody else whose heads are bent like monks in some chilly scriptorium.

"Can I put my money in with yours?" he asks.

"We're not doing laundry here, pal. You're on your own."

"Aw, c'mon."

She hates the supplication. Her dad did that. Pleaded.

She gets in line. He's standing behind her. Too close.

Margaux bets, turns away. Takes in the huge banners with jockeys' pictures hanging from the ceiling. Today's top three or four riders. Plus Shoemaker and Arcaro: the legends.

It's less than a minute to the post. She leads the way out front. He's dying to talk. Make her laugh. Get her going. Score some points. Boys make her feel like she's in a video game, one with a lot of twists and turns, caverns and blind alleys. And when they win, she loses.

She holds an index finger to her lips: Shhhhh. She likes to feel the crowd banked like a fire, but ready to burst into flame.

Then they're off.

"Are we winning?" He bounces up and down, tassels lashing his loafers. "Are we winning?"

In fact, they are. Margaux can see the cherry silks of Brutal Interlude, moving smoothly four wide but in the clear. They're a long way from the turn, but she knows what's happening. She used to stand down there and watch the thoroughbreds change leads, lay back their ears, and go for the wire.

"Is that him? Were we first?"

"Yes."

"All right!"

She warns him, "Don't even think about picking me up and swinging me around. This isn't an Adam Sandler movie."

"What'd we win? How much?"

Margaux glances at the board. "How much did you bet?"

"Like twenty dollars."

"Now you've got almost two hundred."

"Let's do it again." He reaches for her hand.

"I'll meet you by the walking ring," she tells him. "I'm going to the bathroom."

Downstairs she washes her face, glances in the mirror. She's the best-looking girl at the track. Hands down.

There's a racing newspaper on the green couch. She sits and finds the next race. Each horse has a biography of its own. A curriculum vitae. Some are chronicles of success; others are case studies for the indifferent or injured. She looks for the latter.

Mr. You Know Who waits outside, nursing a cocksure grin.

"Let's scope out these horses." He uses her very words, and Margaux wants to kick him.

She can hear her dad. "Pick me a winner, sweetheart." He never asked unless he was desperate. Which is what led to those episodes with Tony.

"Which one this time?" He whispers in her ear because he figures it's time for that. And it turns her on a little. Despite herself. Even under these circumstances. The body as traitor. The body as foe.

"Number seven. Winter Dream."

He's a mild-looking old gelding. This is his job. He's done it almost a hundred times.

"Are you sure? This is the race where I'm supposed to bet Big Max."

"Have I been wrong yet?"

She leads him to the windows. Gets behind him this time.

She watches him fidget in line. He starts glancing over his shoulder, making sure she's there. Huge grins. If there's anything she hates, it's little-boy qualities.

When it's her turn, she pretends to bet.

Minutes later, one arm slithers around her shoulders and she doesn't shrug it away. "How much," he asks, "are we gonna win?"

"Winter Dream is twenty-to-one. That's forty for two dollars. Four hundred for twenty. You bet it all back, didn't you?"

His eyes get wide. "For sure." She sees the movie he's running: dinner someplace he's only driven past, stories about his high school, a secret or two, the usual ridiculous wooing. He blurts, "I live with my mother still."

"Honesty's the best policy."

Like Margaux knew he would, Winter Dream

runs fourth almost all the way. Then he tires in the lane and finishes sixth.

Her companion is stunned. "We didn't win. Big Max did."

"I gotta go."

"What? No. Wait."

She turns, walks away, waiting to hear the name he'll call her.

"You bitch! I heard you were a bitch!"

In her apartment building's forsaken parking lot (potholes, cars with flat tires, broken-down RVs), she pulls in beside the neighbor's boat and cries. Just puts her forehead against the steering wheel and sobs. Then reaches in the back, finds a book, opens at random, and immediately feels a little better.

She likes those cartoons about someone on a tiny island: one palm tree, a keg of water. The endless variations of it. Let's add a carton of books. She in tattered clothes, coconut for breakfast, shade, a novel she's read only a dozen times. When a ship appears, it's a big one with a casino. Couples in gaudy hats and streamers lining the rail clutching the complimentary margarita. She hears the band playing "Proud Mary," and decides not to light the signal fire after all.

Margaux climbs out of the Mustang, closes the door behind her. It's five o'clock, maybe five-thirty. Smog makes the setting sun a deeper red, the color of some internal organ.

She's thinking about mythology, about reluctant Daphne/relentless Apollo, as she gets her things out of the car that Daddy bought. It's bright red. He liked it, thought it was just the ticket. Sporty, spunky, peachy keen. And Margaux? It reminds her of a wound.

Margaux wonders if she could, as Daphne did, cry out to Mother Earth for protection. And have every suitor find a laurel tree in his arms. People would still look up to her (ha, ha). Misjudge her. Misunderstand her. Worship her even (those damn Druids). Or carve someone else's name into her.

Then there's the personalized license plate: BETRAYD. Dad wanted BIGRED; he thought that was cute. But she filled in the blanks on the application. And by the time it came, he'd forgotten. The Derby was coming up. Or a Texas Hold 'Em tourney in Gardena.

She likes the license plate. It's her car. Hadn't she closed the deal herself, sweet-talking the sales-child (no way was he a man) while Dad held out twenty-five thousand dollars in cash he'd won not two hours earlier?

Wearily she climbs the precarious stairs of the Norton Apartments.

Her dad is home. On the couch with Mom. They've been making out, and both look up guiltily when Margaux comes in.

"Doesn't anybody knock anymore?" Mom asks.

"I live here."

"Where've you been?" Her dad has a joint, which he holds out, lighted end down, as if he were passing her a handgun.

She waves it away. "The track."

"Running or racing?"

"Racing."

That gets his attention. He sits straight up like those prairie dogs on the Animal Channel. "Your mom and I had lunch in the Club House. Why didn't you stop by?"

"Get serious."

"Make any money?"

Margaux lies. "No." Then she doesn't lie. "I hate that place." She goes to the sink, runs water into cupped hands, splashes it onto her swollen eyes.

"Well, that's nice," her mother says. "That's appetizing."

Her father stands. "We were going to eat. Want to eat?"

"Doesn't he look nice, Margaux?" Her mother points. "Those are two-hundred-dollar pants."

Everything her dad bought at the deli is in its own clear plastic container. He arranges these on the table in two short rows, like houses in a subdivision. Eight little glass houses. Mr. and Mrs. Potato Salad. Ms. Waldorf. The Ravioli brothers. None of whom should throw stones.

His apron says KISS THE COOK. All he's doing is taking lids off containers, but he doesn't want spots on his linen shirt, blue-gray like smoke from a locomotive. He takes a miniature ear of corn out of a container, looks at it, and scowls like a baffled farmer. Then hands her a blue plate. There's a little egg yolk (or something jaundiced) baked on. She can't believe how good the food looks. How hungry she is. She wants to shoot her needy body. Not herself. Just her body.

She watches her father. On his plate, he has a quartet of helpings. Four little huts. He grins. Not the grin that gets the cocktail waitress every time. Not the smug one when he comes home with twelve grand. This one's soft and nostalgic. Rueful. "As I remember, sweetheart, you and I had a pretty good time at the races when you were little."

Margaux stares, incredulous. She bolts for the bathroom and throws up bile. Then she flees.

Twenty minutes later, she's in the gym. Here's the desk behind which stands a son of Zeus, the same one who, as she returned the membership paperwork and took out her Visa card that first day, waved it away, saying, "Oh, please. People are going to join just to watch you work out."

Once changed, she has to decide where to begin. Let's see—the Bollinger Total Body Ball? Incline bench? Chest press, seated leg press, standing leg press, levitating leg press, dip station, pec dec, Godlike Glutes, Bowflex, More Lithe Than Thou, StairMaster, StairMistress, or maybe just some tools of self-loathing and disappointment like the Fast Track digital body fat calipers or the Omron body fat analyzer?

Everything gleams; everything is wiped off constantly by some employee whose thighs might look like graven images and whose shoulders are so wide they're wingspan. But not their waists. Those are no bigger around than a cake. And the members gleam, too, all with the prescribed patina, augmented by designer water and T-shirts that say they've been to Cancún, Prague, the rings of Saturn.

There's no stubble here, no cellulite. No stains on spandex, no scuffed shoes or socks that have seen better days. No broken symmetry or slowly surfacing fears. Everyone listens to the piped-in music, pitched to the heartbeat of a frightened eland. Their talk is always—summer or winter—about lift tickets. Both literal and symbolic.

She mounts a new machine, the Juno Wheel, as someone in a blue smock comes out of the women's restroom. She's carrying a blue plastic bucket (does it match her smock on purpose?), a toilet brush, and a bottle of Simple Green. Ah, she's the one who works here, who vacuums one-handed. Sleepy. Going over the same foot of carpet. Then she does the baseboards. Everyone else lunges, thrusts, squats, and groans. This one kneels and sighs.

There's something about it that makes Margaux run faster and farther. Climb enough imaginary stairs to reach the ionosphere. Then grab a towel, one of the ten million available, piled high like the mattresses in that fairy tale about the princess and the pea.

The locker room is almost deserted. She sheds both shoes and socks, then lies down on the wide bench, using the towel as a pillow. Tries to get her breathing under control. She hears the whisper of other soles. The slight creak of wood.

"Your feet are perfect, kid. How do you do it?"

She opens her eyes. The new neighbor is all in green: an athletic vegetable. But she's had a lot of work done. Her face is tight. Her forehead never moves. Pillowy lips. But George Washington hands that cannot tell a lie.

"I, uh, used to go to this salon." Margaux gestures. "You know—manicures, pedicures." *Wonder cures.* Still, this is good. Talking is good.

"Where?"

"Arroyo and California. But I can't go there anymore. Because there are these Vietnamese girls in floppy rubber gloves who never get to stand up because they're always working on somebody's toes. And if that's not bad enough, the hairstylists are all wearing camouflage pants and combat boots just like the soldiers who probably killed those girls' relatives. It's just too weird."

"I don't get it," says her new friend. "They're probably glad to have a job. And it's not like you shot their water buffalo."

After this, she drives until her soul is at least half-tucked into her body. Down half-familiar streets.

Not as tired from the gym as she wants to be. Not nearly tired enough.

Through the open window, the *shush* of sprinklers on better lawns than hers, a jogger with a better dog (if she had a dog), and inside a better house a real room of her own. An add-on for the beloved daughter's sixteenth birthday. A gift with no strings attached. Not one in lieu of. Or as compensation for. Not a bribe. Not hush money or redress.

All of a sudden someone running at top speed darts from between two houses. He's no jogger. She notes his inappropriate shoes and garb: stupid shirt, dumb-ass pants.

It turns into a math problem: if a Ford Mustang is going thirty miles per hour south and a malefactor is going seven miles per hour east, how long before . . .

Then he's right in front of her, arms up like someone trying to stop a train. She brakes. He rockets to the passenger side and tries the door.

"Let me in!"

Under the seat there's a wrench her father gave

her. Just in case. Her fingers tighten around the cool metal handle.

He's not beating on the glass; he's just beseeching. "Will you let me in!? Please."

Wait. She might know this kid. A year behind her in school. A light-year behind her in every other way. He's no felon. He's the animal nut. She's seen him at the mall handing out Humane Society leaflets. Wearing a baseball hat with Pluto ears.

Margaux opens the door. He's in just like that but turned around in the seat, peering out. And not just corkscrewed like someone working hard on his parallel parking skills, but on his knees facing backward like a kid leaving someplace he liked. Or maybe not. Maybe like a kid leaving a place he couldn't stand and enjoyed seeing shrink and disappear.

Margaux views him discretely: little hands, weak chin, a high forehead already, and hair both attenuate and insufficient. Somebody, in short, she could never like. Never in a million years.

But somebody who liked her. Since all the boys liked her. Or said they did. Or Sara said they did.

She says, "Unless you're part of some night-owl track meet, I'll bet you're running away from the cops."

He turns, settles into the seat, reaches for the belt, and pulls it across his almost-certainly concave chest.

"Actually, no."

She notices the hole in his long-sleeved shirt. A very long-sleeved shirt and probably concealing an elbow badly in need of jojoba oil.

She can't imagine where he got those clothes: some giant's shirt, pants dark with toil, big dumb corroded archaic shoes.

"So what were you up to?"

He shows her both hands, fingers apart like a conjuror. "'Tell me, O Muse, of that ingenious hero who traveled far and wide after he had sacked the famous town of Troy.'"

"What?"

"It's the first line of *The Odyssey.* My way of answering your question: maybe I was just traveling far and wide."

"What you were doing was running very fast."

"If you can believe Joseph Campbell, in the hero's journey a guide or helper appears early on. Maybe that's you. Maybe I was running to you."

"That's no answer and you don't look like any hero I ever saw."

He reaches for the rearview mirror. Inspects. Nods. Says with exaggerated sadness, "Too true."

"So c'mon. What were you up to?"

"It's a long story."

"Oh, yeah? Well, what if I just drive around until you tell me?"

"You're not going to do that. Somebody might see us, and then what would you tell Sara?" He points. "And, anyway, my car is right there." He's out quickly. Gracefully. "Thanks. See you around."

"Yeah, see you." She hears a microgram of disappointment. He was a welcome distraction, a new book from the carton on her little island. But he's right: What would she tell Sara?

MORNING. The television is on in the living room. Margaux hears—can't help but hear—a hectoring aerobics instructor, then someone selling a ring, followed by a piping voice from a kids' show, probably delivered by some admonitory dog or stern cow with kind eyes: "Don't believe anyone that tells you they have candy or need help finding a lost puppy."

Margaux mutters into her closet. "It's anyone *who,* not anyone *that.* And it should be *he,* not *they.* Don't believe *him* when *he* says *he* has candy or has lost *his* puppy."

She feels like wearing something ugly, but probably can't. What if she threw on a miserable little jacket, used string to hold up her worst jeans, and carried money and makeup in an argyle sock?

She'd just get her picture in the school paper. Again. Taken by yet another leering shutterbug.

She settles for sandals, pleated linen pants, and a white blouse that coats her torso like frost. Then exits.

"Never," says an actor in a cardigan, "ever go up to a van, especially one with tinted windows."

He's less a man than an inventory of parts: head, chest, stomach, legs, feet. Sexless as a grocery list.

A cow on roller skates glides by carrying a glass of milk.

"Calcium," says Bland Man, "for strong bones and teeth."

"So you can bite your abductor," says Margaux.

"Did we keep you up last night?" Mom asks. Her tone is both coy and insinuating.

Margaux shakes her head. Sara has some pills that make sleep descend like a fine gold net.

There's nothing in the refrigerator but cottage cheese, ketchup, and a huge bully of a watermelon. As Margaux reaches for one of the cartons, her mom warns, "Don't wake your dad."

"With the clamor of cottage cheese?"

"He had a long night." There it is again. That self-congratulatory concupiscence. "Come here, honey." Her mother has one arm out. Does she really expect Margaux to snuggle up to her? "Look at this."

On the screen are three boys and a girl. The latter is lank as a weed with a bikini bottom slung as low as Standards and Practices will permit and puffy, slapped-around cheeks. One of the boys is just some Darrell from Memphis; another is the butcher's apprentice; the third needs a transfusion of some kind.

"Who would you pick, honey? They're all so good-looking."

"I'm late. I'll eat at school." Or not at all.

Margaux has skin the color of flour bleached and milled a hundred times. And skin like that opens doors, paves the way. Especially in her high school.

As she walks among her classmates, some of them fall back like Robin Hood's men catching a glimpse of Maid Marian.

She watches a couple make out, a silver suspension bridge of spit connecting them even when they part. Her stomach gyrates, then balks.

She overhears her peers: "Didja see that car crash, man? That copter explode? That guy on the bike who went over the side, man? Didja see the cops shoot that man, man? Didja see that truck blow up, those bleachers collapse, the bull gore that guy? Didja see it? Didja see it? Didja see it? Are you kiddin'? Well, they're showing it again tonight. I'll come over—we'll get high and tape it, okay?"

By this time she's completely out of her body, floating above the shoals of students, looking down. But not with the divine complacency of those people on that *Other Side* show her mom loves. They—the survived—return after car wrecks and skiing accidents to tell about their ride on some big Sylvania glass-bottomed boat and to report they are no longer afraid of death.

Well, neither is Margaux. It's life that's scary.

"Hey!"

Sara throws her arms around her from behind. She plants half a dozen quick, pizzicato kisses on her cheek.

Blessed Sara, her jabber and pant.

"Margaux, what's this I hear about you and Ned Strand at the racetrack?"

"Is that who that was? Well, let's just say there wasn't magic in the air."

"It doesn't matter. Ned will talk about it forever. He already called like a dozen of his pals."

"I was rude to him."

"Good. He lives with his mother." Sara has wrapped a pearl necklace around her wrist, and it looks great.

"Tomorrow," says Margaux, "half a dozen girls will have pearls around their wrists but it will just look like they can't tell their clavicles from their carpal articulations."

"Babe, are you just entertaining yourself with those big words again, or has your blood sugar dropped all the way down to your pretty feet and you need a bite of this Egg McMuffin?" Sara holds up something in pollen-yellow swaddling. "It's yours. I'm only carrying it because it matches my purse." A quick nudge toward some poor sophomore. "And speaking of a fashion no-no, get a load of her kicks. Are those pathetic knockoffs or what?"

"Those are facsimiles of counterfeit misrepresentations. Those are distortions of a bad likeness to begin with."

Sara grins. "They might be all right if she was fifty and her husband died."

"And she joined a lesbian commune in Colorado."

"But definitely not now."

"Definitely not today, October twenty-second in the year of our lard."

"And speaking of lard, see you at lunch, sweet cheeks." One kiss and she's gone.

Margaux likes to lean into the mean wind that is Sara. And when she is suddenly on her own, abandoned, left to her own devices, she's all aslant. Then, thank God, he comes by — last night's benign highwayman.

He's wearing weird shoes, too. These look like loaves of bread made by Simpleton Bakery (Kakes and Pyes 4 Awl Okayshuns). A T-shirt and painters' pants. Real painters' pants. With paint on them. Lots of it. So much that they look like a carapace.

God, maybe he's on the cutting edge, after all. Beyond the edge, in some alternate fashion universe. In six months, she might steal those pants or, as Sara likes to do, take them into a dressing room and with her own little scissors snip holes in them.

"Hey!"

He slows, makes a deliberate turn, looking over one shoulder like someone with only a learner's permit. "Hey, yourself."

"What's your name, anyway?"

"Danny Riley."

"I'm—"

"Everybody knows you." But without any paramour topspin, much less servile homage.

Just then a tsunami of athletes sweeps down the hall (Go, Wolverines!). Margaux and Danny step aside, flattening themselves against the Bowery-colored wall. He's surprisingly light on his feet. When it's over, students peer out of doorways, drift back into the hall, blinking and peering about like survivors.

Danny just stands. His silence disarms her. She's used to boys chattering away, complimenting her, joking with her, offering things—a kind of rapid-fire sharpshooting that clips buttons off her dress, shatters buckles, and leaves her standing in stolen underwear while they take a bow.

She asks, "What was all that about last night, Danny Riley?"

"I was just checking on one of my dogs."

"One of your what?"

"I work for the Humane Society."

"I've seen you in that wonderful hat. The one with the ears."

He has a grin that is like a premonition of a grin. He uses that. "When people adopt animals," he explains, "we get their names and addresses. Then I go by and make sure everything's okay."

"And you got the night shift?"

"Sort of."

"Who was chasing you?"

"Probably somebody who thought I was a prowler; I was kind of hanging over his fence. Whoever it was had a gun, I think."

"Seriously?"

"Or a pork chop. It was dark."

He tries to casually put a hand in one pocket,

but it's painted shut. His palm skids away, like a car that tries to tuck itself into its own garage but hits a patch of ice.

"Where did you get those pants?"

"Somebody threw them away."

"No kidding."

"They're perfectly good pants." He points to the Egg McMuffin still in her hand. "If you're not going to eat that . . ."

She holds it out.

"Thanks. I gotta go. I don't believe in being tardy."

Not even one Orphean over-the-shoulder glance like the others? Well, that was different.

Impressed (but why?), she watches him until he's swallowed up by scurrying students. Soon she's alone in those polished corridors except for one monitor, a boy wearing heavy pants and a heavy matching vest. Ruddy, he looks like he might pop out of some Tyrolean clock to announce the hour.

"I'm just going to the office"—she glances at his plastic nametag—"Justin."

"Absolutely." Stay overnight. Eat breakfast. Love me forever.

The overhead lights in said office buzz. Everybody who works there squints: Mrs. Flare, Ms. Maiden Name, Mrs. Upper-Left-Hand Corner, Ms. Nothing Can Console Me.

Margaux beckons a student assistant. "I need you to break a rule for me"—another nametag glance—"Shannon."

"Gee, I don't know."

"Shannon, Shannon, are you really willing to forgo the pleasures of mutiny?"

Mutiny. The word allows Shannon to picture herself in tattered shorts, tall boots, and a cutlass. First mate of the good ship Dexatrim.

"What kind of rule?"

Margaux leans in so Shannon can smell her, because she is redolent of mown grass, lilacs, and something not quite graspable but much to be desired. "I just need Danny Riley's address."

"Danny Riley." Followed by both a question mark and an exclamation. Or two.

"I borrowed a book, and I don't particularly want to see him again. I thought I'd just drop it by his house. Maybe toss it on the lawn like a newspaper."

Shannon bellows, "I can find that information for you."

She's trying too hard and everyone looks up, even Principal Antimatter.

The other clerks/typists/serfs—the real ones, not the student aides, but the lifers—glance at Margaux. They are like everybody else, just as heliotropic; their faces turned toward Margaux's luminosity. One of them, Ms. Maiden Name, has a new dress. A frock. And just as she is about to see what that Shannon is up to, Margaux intercepts her.

"That's the perfect color for you."

Ms. M.N. rises halfway out of her chair and—there's no other word for this—curtsies.

Shannon returns with a slip of paper. She smiles conspiratorially. Twists that into a smirk befitting someone as suddenly Machiavellian as she.

Margaux palms the note and says, "You're a slyboots."

That compliment makes Shannon laugh out loud with pleasure. The clerks smile. The principal reaches into his desk for a bonbon. Really. An honest-to-God bonbon. Which he keeps there for moments like this, when everything seems to be going particularly well.

THAT NIGHT at home, the big TV in the living room is on; ditto the little one on the no-doubt bacteria-riddled counter in the kitchen. Neither is turned up loud, but it's still some kind of addled stereo, a foul stream muttering its way to a polluted river.

Dinner is macaroni and cheese. The latter is radiation-alert orange, a color Margaux has seen only in discount stores and usually on a rack of stretch pants. Stores where Sara tracks the demise of one or another cultural/fashion trend.

Her mother points to the small screen: "Who would order an extra-large muumuu in brown?

You'd look like a yurt." She glances at her daughter. "Didn't think I knew that word, did you?"

"Brown?" (What a bitch she is.)

"*Yurt,* Miss Perfect Pants. I learned that today. Watching the Travel Channel."

Click.

"This system," says a Weather Channel mannequin, "already has a history of damage."

"Do you think he's cute, honey?"

"No." Margaux pokes at her dinner. There's macaroni that one eats and there's macaronies meaning the affected Brits of the eighteenth century. That's the reference in "Yankee Doodle Dandy": not someone with pasta in his hat but ostentation/pretension.

How language comforts her! A thesaurus is soothing as a Bible. More. Those families of words: the mom and pop, the offspring, nieces and nephews, and toward the bottom of the page a kinsman twice removed whom no one exactly understands, but a place at the table is found for him anyway.

"Margaux."

"I said no. I don't think he's good-looking."

"That's a nice suit."

"It's stupid, Mom. It's a disguise."

After a brief inspection: "Gee, it is, isn't it? I never thought about it before, honey. But you're right. Just because he's dressed up like a nice young man doesn't mean he is."

Her mother can do this sometimes: drop the sniping, the innuendo, the chipping away, the general dispersal of blight, yearning, and envy.

The weatherman is only too glad to try out his apocalyptic voice: "And those of you in Henley County are going to want to avoid windows and find some shelter downstairs, preferably in the southeast corner."

That's when the phone rings. Her mother picks up, listens, says, "Oh. . . . Oh. . . . Oh. . . . Oh."

She might be an actress with a very small part. One word, actually. But she practices anyway, putting a sympathetic spin on it. Then interrogative, followed by agitated and acquiescent.

"I'll do it right now. Margaux will take me."

She hangs up. Looks at her daughter. "We need to wire your dad some money."

"I thought he was playing cards downtown."

"He was losing in California, so he flew to Vegas."

Margaux fast-forwards the argument: *Oh, Mom./ Don't be that way, honey. You know I hate to drive by myself/furthermore/ad infinitum/besides/et cetera.*

She reaches for her keys, which dangle from a giant 7, souvenir of Nevada, where she has never been. Will never go.

Her mother stands, looks down at herself. "Can I wear these pants? When I ordered them, the lady said they were a durable fabric in a freedom-inspiring style that was both street-smart and trail-wise."

"They're fine, Mom."

"I'll just get the money."

Alone, Margaux gulps water. That her mother remembered the sales pitch word for word is wrenching. She pictures her on the phone, credit card at the ready, talking to the clerk, Blanche, her new friend.

When she starts to feel lightheaded, Margaux slaps herself. Hard. *Stop that!* Then leans into the sink and washes her face.

Mom comes out of the bedroom with a bowl of money (where did that come from?), loose hundreds tossed like a salad. She counts out twenty into a pile. Offers Margaux a couple. Which she accepts. *(I'm earning this.)*

"Let's take your car, sweetheart. You know how I am. And lock the doors."

They navigate evening streets: past a Mexican restaurant hung with Chinese lanterns; a hamburger joint alfresco where the chairs nearest the curb lie on their sides, legs out like dead animals; and finally a pocket-sized park featuring—in the daytime, at any rate—a waterfall, a hill, two winding paths that intersect, a brook. At night, however, high-school kids frequent that toy Eden to deal drugs and tease the bold koi.

Outside Western Union, Margaux parks beside

a wall wretched with graffiti: an original prankster or two, a bouquet of monikers (Tudy, Oso, Chato), a hundred boasts rubbed out, repainted, rubbed out again: I'M THE BEST. THERE'S NOTHING YOU CAN DO ABOUT IT. 187 everywhere, the penal-code number for murder.

Her mother won't get out of the car; she wants to listen to a tape of Tibetan chants, which came with a meditation turtleneck that was too small.

Inside, Margaux has to wait in line. Two feral children eye her. In a corner lies a dog with an outsized head. There's an old woman turning over cards and muttering. It's like some spirit world of folk art, a scene painted on tin by a crippled miner. With Margaux as the centerpiece, light streaming out of her ears.

Finally it's her turn. The clerk's T-shirt reads SHOCK THE MONKEY. He does the paperwork, then oozes, "Boyfriend in trouble?"

"It's for my dad. He's got cancer."

Smirk, smirk. "In Las Vegas?"

"Las Vegas is the cancer capital of the world."

Outside, she turns down the tape *("Om mane padme om")*, the one her mother isn't listening to anyway. She's bent over some women's magazine, reading an article called "Is It Love or Lust? Six Sure-fire Ways to Tell the Difference!"

"Mom, do you ever feel like you're going crazy?"

"Oh, sweetie. Don't take things so seriously: the world is your oyster."

Just as she suspected: the world is something slimy in a shell.

"Why did you marry Dad, anyway?"

"Are you kidding? He's gorgeous."

"He's a creep."

"You watch your mouth, young lady. He's still your father."

"When I was ten — "

Her mother actually does something Margaux has seen only on TV. She puts an index finger in each ear and begins to yodel. Like one of the monkeys in that famous trio of monkeys, she wants to hear no evil. There's plenty of evil to hear, too.

And Margaux has tried to tell her before. But she won't try again.

Half an hour later, Margaux finds herself squinting at Danny's address on Purdy Street, then at the house with a big curving porch and shake roof. Purdy. A kid's way of saying pretty. And it is pretty: puddles stippled by automatic sprinkler systems, yet no dregs in the gutters as on her block. A few cars at the curb but fat, radiant ones. Somebody walking a dog, and that somebody's running shoes are white as the trim on Santa's cuffs.

Up the walk she goes, between the agapanthus and the dusty heather. Mounting five steps (not the contingent ramp), skirting sun-and-moon wind chimes, right to the broad door with its brass knocker, which she uses almost discreetly because she's not knocking but tapping, gently rapping like that famous raven in the Poe poem. Not thunderous or fisty, not even insistent, but steady. Regular but not monotonous. Determined and unflagging.

So, of course, the door opens and there he is.

Danny Riley. In his fallen-down clothes: a red and black lumberjack shirt tonight, two hundred times too big for him. Pants—what she can see of them—a kind of something-in-a-petri-dish green. Barefoot. Pale, delicate feet. Idealistic feet.

"Hey. What's up?"

He's not stunned to find her at his door. Not flustered. Not flattered or flummoxed. Just, "Hey. What's up?" Most natural thing in the world.

She leans forward: this is urgent. "Next time you have to check on some dogs, take me with you, okay?"

"Good timing. I was just on my way out."

"Now?"

"Yeah. Come on in."

Relieved. Grateful. *(But why, exactly?)* She follows him into the living room: polished hardwood floors, no carpet, a low round coffee table strewn with magazines, ceiling-to-floor bookcases, a woman in a wheelchair.

"Aunt Evie, this is Margaux. With an *x*. Margaux, this is Evie. Short for Evelyn."

Margaux likes his chivalry, both mock and

earnest. Mock-earnest. Evie clutches a wineglass with both hands like it's a grail.

She says, "MS. Multiple sclerosis."

Margaux looks puzzled.

"Is what I've got," says Evelyn. "I just tell people right off. And that it does come and go, but this time it seems to have signed a lease and called the cable guy." A shrug. Then a knotty smile. "Can I get you something?"

Danny answers for her. "We're kind of going someplace. I'll just put on some shoes."

Now she's alone with Evelyn. Evie in a white turtleneck and purple pants with a stretch waistband. Her hair—lots of it—is cut by someone who knows what he/she is doing. Margaux tries to imagine going to a salon in a wheelchair. Can't.

Silence makes Margaux nervous. Makes her want to smile too much. Talk too much. Babble.

Where do you work?

Have you read all these books?

Isn't the weather lovely?

Where's Danny's mom and dad?

Evie finishes her wine and begins, "What's wrong with your dog, Margaux?"

"I don't have a dog."

Evie leans forward. "Everybody who comes through that door has a dog. It's a kind of ticket."

"We're classmates sort of. He's a year behind me."

"Are you sure you don't have a dog? Not out in the car? Not a little bitty one in your purse?"

"No."

"Are you working on a school project together?"

"No."

"He has some notes or homework that you missed."

"No."

"You just dropped by."

"I gave him a ride the other night and . . ." She can't finish.

"He left something in your car."

She shakes her head. "I don't really know why I'm here."

"Now we're getting somewhere."

"Maybe I just followed him home."

"Hoping he'd keep you? I doubt it. If nothing else, you two are, shall we say, at opposite ends of the fashion seesaw."

"Or shall we say antipodal. For brevity's sake. And accuracy's."

Evelyn looks her over, scans her, re-evaluates her. Margaux can almost see the calibrations. Then Evelyn licks a finger. Makes an invisible mark on the air. "Score one for you."

Danny ambles in. "What's going on? It feels a little charged up out here."

"Girl talk," says Evie.

"Margaux?"

"We're fine."

Danny leans, kisses Evie's cheek. Her hand comes up, holds his face to hers for a moment. Then he says to Margaux, "Ready?"

No. Despite inquisitorial Evelyn, she likes it here. Reading lamps like big drooping flowers. The tall and learned precincts of these four walls. Light that is almost edible. People who don't just whine and brag. People who don't just hand out hundred-dollar bills or watch TV sixteen hours a day. People who don't put their daughters in jeopardy.

"Okay. Sure."

Evie rolls closer. Takes one of her hands. "It was a pleasure."

She meets Evelyn's wary, large-irised eyes. She says, "Seriously?"

"I don't have time to say things I don't mean, kiddo."

Outside, Margaux says, "I don't think your aunt likes me."

"Today wasn't a good day for first impressions. She had to go to the doctor, and the numbers weren't what she hoped they'd be."

"What numbers?"

"Blood tests, stuff like that. So when we got home, she had a few glasses of wine." He puts both arms out, sways a little. "Do you ever think you can feel the earth turn?"

Is there a right answer to this? One he expects to hear? One he'd prefer?

He glances down. "Do you ever think of all the animals underneath?"

"Underneath?"

"Yeah. Ones with big, leathery wings. And tusks and stuff like that. Rotting away."

"I've been too busy thinking about how I look."

Danny waves one hand, as if to disperse the bees of self-contempt that fly out of her mouth.

"It can't take that much time, can it? You're naturally pretty."

That may be the most impartial evaluation of her beauty she's ever heard. Why isn't he stunned by her, like every other guy in the world?

"Do you want me to drive?" she asks, half-insulted, half-flattered.

"We're probably better off in my car." He opens the garage door to reveal a blue Porsche convertible and . . . and a . . . well, something else. Which he walks toward. Then strolls around to open the door on the passenger's side. Her side.

There's no irony, no subtext, no ulterior motive. He's just polite.

She slides in. "What kind of ride is this, anyway?"

"A Mercury Sable. What color would you say it is?"

"I don't know. Ashen?"

When he smiles, she feels like she's accomplished something.

"A good color," he says, "for a getaway car. Better, no offense, than your incarnadine Mustang."

She loves that he knows that word, has seen it in context, looked it up or divined its meaning, remembered it, found a place for it talking to her.

She waits until he's inside, too. "Who drives the Porsche?"

"Evie used to. Not anymore. Now put on your seat belt, okay? Better safe than sorry."

Margaux entertains a question she's never asked/never had to ask/never felt like asking a boy in her life. *Are you glad I'm here?* Clearly the others were glad: the compliments, the fawning, the plans they laid. Their excursions and jaunts, their itineraries, projects, stratagems, and schemes.

What about this one?

They drive through moon-drenched streets: navigate a penniless block or two, a land of bundles, environ of the suspicious glance, outpost of the night shift, the shore of survivors, Prodigal Son Boulevard.

Eventually, he glides to the curb, turns off the lights and ignition. The cooling engine gives off little insect-clicks.

"Ready?" he asks.

She has her head down, but conscious of the way her hair falls across one (the left) flawless cheek.

"I don't know why I want to do this," she blurts, "but I do."

"Yeah, I know what you mean. It's not like we're getting paid. But since we're here, just remember: If we have to run for it, I'm leaving the keys in the car."

He makes what they're doing sound dangerous but noble. Like shoplifting for the indigent.

"We're just checking on adopted dogs, right?"

"Right."

"Why don't we just go to the door and ask?"

"The owners say, 'Come back tomorrow.' By then the dog's got water and a new collar." He takes a deep breath. "So, one more time: If we get separated and you get back here first, take the car. I'll be fine. But if it's the other way around, I'll wait for you."

I'll wait for you. That's more like it. Except he doesn't mean it in that Knights of the Round Table/Heathcliff and Cathy kind of way. He's more like Lassie.

She closes the door on her side, meets him on the sidewalk. This is an intermediate neighborhood—not as good as his, better than hers, which means no kids' toys to garnish a balding lawn, but there is a camper or two and at least one boat-on-a-trailer.

"Act natural," he says, setting off.

"So I should be a haughty bitch?"

He puts one cautionary finger to his lips. "Shhhh."

They walk between houses, cut through a backyard, and dodge a homemade skateboard ramp, a swing set, a small freestanding pool, and—swimming in it—one solitary duck.

At the sight of that, Danny grins at her and she grins back.

They creep through a denuded backyard: grass ripped out, earth worked over then raked and smoothed, probably by those men who congregate at the rent-a-truck place, those men who—when she passes—eye her hungrily not because she's "pretty" but because they want to carry, tote, lift, shove, push, hammer, douse, whap, swat, and/or scrub anything for six dollars an hour.

And her father's work? Somewhere he holds a little geisha's fan (jack, queen, king, ace, seven) or sits in air-conditioned comfort watching thoroughbreds hurl themselves from a starting gate.

And Mother? Click—"Five easy payments." Click—"Oh, Paul, your music will always come first." Click—"Lose twenty-five pounds by Thanksgiving."

"We're almost there. Watch the cacti."

He would know the plural.

She has no idea where she is. Though it occurs

to her—comforts her—that she could go to the door of any lighted house and knock. When they saw her through the peephole or past the little chain, they'd let her in. Because she was young and beautiful and a girl. Who was lost.

He tugs at her, and they go to their knees beside a hedge of oleanders.

"Don't get these in your mouth," he cautions, "they're poisonous." Parting the thick stems, he whistles softly, then calls, "Here, Blue."

One cautionary *woof!* Then the damp snuffle of a big dog.

"Blue! How are you, girl? Are you fine?"

He leaves entirely, steps through the oleanders and disappears. Behind her is a collection of cacti in big, black, plastic pots. Eventually they'll be put into the ground at attractive intervals, but now they're massed as if for an attack.

Margaux grins. She's having a good time. She's excited and alert. Sure, she's surprised Danny doesn't hit on her, but if he did, she'd have nothing but scorn for him.

"C'mon, Margaux. It's okay."

He sounds like Superman or Perry Mason talking to Lois Lane or Della Street. Those men (one man, actually, and one Man of Steel) would never grope and moan. Nor would Danny.

She parts the oleanders, wriggles through, stands up.

"Say hi to Blue."

She's a big, dark Lab with a tongue as thick as a blackjack. And a lot wetter.

"You look good," Danny says, animated now. Emancipated, sort of. (But from what?) Enlarged, maybe, by Blue's eagerness and apparent well-being.

He takes the dog's big head between both hands, puts his nose against hers, and talks baby talk, puppy talk, dog talk.

Margaux remembers the boys who've put that two-handed move on her. Having seen it at the movies or on TV, they know how the kissee always deliquesced. For Margaux, however, it felt like her head was in a vice no matter how leading-man-tenderly it was done. God, always someone leaning over her, eyes closed, mouth open, as if she were a public drinking fountain.

"Everything's fine," Danny says after another minute or two of palpation. "When Blue came to the shelter, she was pretty roughed up, but she got lucky with these new owners. Let's get out of here." He points. "We can go that way. It's a little easier."

They walk side by side — chums, companions, shipmates on leave — toward some street, because Margaux can see drooping arc lights in the distance.

They emerge at the rear of a low one-story apartment building, cut through an empty ramada, and amble (they're loose now, relaxed; mission accomplished) up the long macadam drive that leads from the parking lot to the street.

Margaux can't help but glance into the windows that line this byway like paintings hung in some urban gallery, paintings in a Squalor Series: *Unmade Bed; Exercycle & Unmade Bed; Crib, Unmade Bed, & Giant TV; Unmade Bed With Recumbent Figure; Unmade Bed & False Euphoria.*

She grabs Danny, seizes him, actually, so maybe that's why he flinches and pulls away. She whispers, "Want to see something sexy?" Hearing even as she says it all the *s*'s with their inevitable viperish connotations.

"You go ahead." Danny turns away. Not just back toward the street, either, but further by many degrees.

So she does "go ahead" and peers into a room dark as gunpowder. In the foreground stands a Tinkertoy high-rise all askance. And beyond that . . . Margaux balks. Why is she doing this? She doesn't want to see the immodest choreography on that bed. Not really. Sara would. Sara wants to see everything. But she's not Sara. So is it time to stop acting like Sara?

Danny has both hands in his pockets like a man about to whistle. A car mutters down the drive, angles away from them, and Danny gives a neighborly wave.

They emerge on a street/the street/some street. Half a block or so away is his car, and he was right: it's an indeterminate color. Gray, maybe. Or blue.

Ish. Bluish, smoky. Sort of. A getaway car to get away in.

And what if they had to flee? Would the cops chase them? Would he duck into a bosky lane and she'd have to kiss him like in the movies? Man on the run in Budapest. Double agent Veronica seizes him, tugs him into a doorway, plants one on him as the stupid police clatter past. What would that be like, the kissing part? He's still plain as a board fence; his lips are thin as a cat's.

They make two more stops — checking up on a nervous cocker spaniel and a lethargic beagle. Then they drive in silence back to his house. He walks her to the Mustang, parked at the curb. This is where any other boy in the world would put the moves on her.

He holds out one hand. "Drive carefully."

Margaux laughs. Can't help herself. *Drive carefully?* "When," she asks, "are you going to do this again?"

"I don't know. It depends."

"Can I go? I mean, was I in the way or anything?"

"No, you were fine. I was glad for the company."

"So I can go."

"Sure."

"But you don't know when. Exactly."

"It depends. Pretty soon, probably."

"You could call me, though. When you know."

"Sure."

"Great. How are you going to do that?"

"How am I going to call you?"

"Yeah."

"On the phone?" He sounds like somebody woefully equipped for this pop quiz.

"You'd need my number."

"Oh, sure."

She reaches into her purse, scrawls on the back of a hall pass, hands it over.

He opens the door. "I'll just wait until, you know, your car starts and you get safely on your way."

"You're totally serious, aren't you?"

He's pale as smoke in the moonlight. "About what?"

AT SCHOOL the next day, Margaux looks for Danny/is afraid he's looking for her/wants to see him/wants to avoid him/wonders why he hasn't sought her out/is afraid he will. Really, what can she be thinking: that uncomely face, the spindle-shanked meagerness of him, the teakettle thinness of his breath. His daunting goodness.

And then a boy named Lincoln slinks by, a boy she used to go with in tenth grade. He was really cute, and Sara said they looked great together. Then he was just stupid and vain. Now he's a perfidious reptile. And a semiserious druggie.

"Margaux!" Lincoln never just speaks, never just says. He blurts and howls. "You look great."

"I just got some sleep is all."

"Not me, babe. I was out half the night."

He's so proud of his knavery. Okay, she's been vainglorious about her little sins, too, but she's tired of that. Tired of hearing about it. From him, from herself, from everybody.

Lincoln leans in; his breath smells like a butcher's back pocket. "Don't you want details?"

"Later."

Isn't it odd she can't just—as one of the presidents' wives advised—"say no." Though she wants to. In a way. She planned to, thought she was going to. But then said, "Later." Hedging her bets, perhaps. Not burning her bridges, but at least buying matches and starting to gather kindling. She felt like an entirely different person last night. One her friends would not like; in fact, one they would barely recognize.

Then down the hall—that narrow veldt of trumpeting humanity—comes Sara in black high-tops, inevitable red shorts, and a Dodgers T-shirt.

"'Modesty,'" Margaux says, remembering her French teacher's fondness for Flaubert, "'woman's greatest jewel.'"

"Are they tight enough?" Sara turns.

"You win. You've got a cuter butt."

"Cuter than . . ."

"Aphrodite's."

"And she is . . ."

"Goddess of love and beauty. She had a magic belt, and when she wore it, everybody loved her."

Sara nods. "I had a pair of shoes like that once."

"That's where the word *aphrodisiac* comes from: something that makes you love somebody whether you want to or not."

Well, isn't that an odd thing to say. She doesn't love anybody.

Sara throws an arm around her, kisses her on the cheek. "You know the weirdest things. And speaking of weird things: What were you doing with King of the Urchins last night?"

"How'd you know about that?"

Sara shows her ten Dragon Lady fingernails. "My spies are everywhere."

"I was just helping him with something."

"Did the judge tell you it was either that or pick up trash along the freeway?"

"Danny's okay."

"For somebody who lives under a bridge." Sara runs both hands through her hair. "Listen up, we're going out tonight."

"There's a segue that gives me pause."

"A couple of guys from St. Luke's. Yours already knows where you live."

"But the other one doesn't?"

"Well, no."

"I'll take him."

"Yours is really cute."

"What a surprise."

Sara backs away, "Mega-cute. And a great kisser." From halfway down the hall she announces, "Believe me, I know. Be ready at five, okay?"

And then here's Danny Riley, dressed like a grimy ghost in those painters' pants and something that was once white and is still enormous.

"Where," she asks, "did you get that thing you're wearing?"

Danny glances down. "You don't like this shirt?"

"It looks like a shroud from the Big 'N Tall Shop."

"It's a perfectly good shirt. One hundred percent cotton."

"You really don't care what people think, do you?"

He considers the question. Which disarms her. One of the things she likes—one of the things she's good at — is turbocharged persiflage. But this one thinks before he opens his mouth.

Finally he just shrugs. "I say I don't care, but Evie says it's my way of getting a little attention." He pushes back some unexceptional hair. "Do you believe there's somebody just like you somewhere else?"

Where is this going? Intrigued, she hedges. "Maybe."

"You know what I'm talking about, right? Not a biological twin but a double. Perfect in every detail. See her on the street, freak you right out."

"Keep talking."

"I think mine's got a suntan and a passport, one of those cool ones that looks like it's almost been torn apart by bandits."

"We were talking about how you don't care what people think."

"Right. I'm saying I don't. Evie says I do in a kind of backwards way. But this friendly doppelganger is beyond that. He gets all the attention he wants because he fits in. And he fits in because he's just a regular guy."

"With a tan."

"Right. From volleyball or tennis." He leans toward her as some kids rattle by, then retreats. "How about yours?"

"My double."

"Yes."

Two boys with huge backpacks stop and look at Margaux; three girls chatter at each other and make a big deal of not looking. Then she says, "She'd be modest."

"And?"

"Live in a nice house."

"And?"

"Her parents would love her."

He opens a notebook, sketches quickly. Roughly. "There'd be a deck on the house, okay?"

"Sure."

His pencil lands here and there. "And at night there'd be fireflies."

Just then the bell rings, and he's off. Mr. Never Even Tardy.

* * *

After school, Sara wants to get high, but Margaux demurs. Motion is her drug of choice. Velocity. Flux. Transit.

She starts out by heading away from the animal shelter, taking city streets east, in the direction of those settlers who gave up: no more canvas on their covered wagons, the oxen already devoured, the horses worn down to shadows. She could do that—give up. Just leave the Golden State and settle somewhere else. Kansas, maybe. Or Missouri. Then get a job doing . . . what—being pretty?

She overtakes a goody truck: frozen treats, Popsicles, Dreamsicles, that kind of thing. Dreamsicle/Dreamcycle: something at the gym. A long waiting list for it. *Please erase your name when you're through dreaming.*

Said truck is on its way home, the driver yawning. It's been all over, raising its prices when it crosses into swanky San Marino, where grown men wander out, flag down the driver. They speak to him in Spanish, used to talking to gardeners, cleaning ladies, busboys. Then they stand around in their Orvis I'm-home-now-and-seriously-relaxing clothes.

They like to ruin their dinner (rueful head shakes to each other). "The wife is going to shoot me." The wife.

She remembers these guys. She used to work for them. They drove her home after the party, showing the movie in their heads: *The Babysitter.*

They all smelled like liquor or after-shave. Or smoke, charred around the edges. "So," they asked, "what do you want to be when you grow up?" She answered, "Not you." They loved that; it let them sneak into the next movie: *The Saucy Babysitter.* A big tip for sass.

And then getting out, she leaned to take the folded bills and let them look down her shirt. A little skin and she had them in the palm of her hand. The pathetic bastards.

So did all that start with Tony? Is that why she's such a spiteful tease? She can't forget those bright lights, venomous music, the insinuating lens. The fear.

God, she's in a bad way. All these memories with their teeth and quills.

So she gives up. Stops pretending. And hurries west at last. On the freeway, then off at Fair Oaks, down Glenarm. She parks, asks to see Danny. Danny Riley. Please.

She waits outside, beside the statue of a noble canine. FAITHFUL, say the words carved in stone. LOYAL. There's a semicircle drive with ten-minute parking. People here and there, cages in hand. Dogs bark constantly.

Then out he comes in his work clothes and tall rubber boots.

"I don't know why I'm here," she blurts.

"Gee, Evie and I were talking about that just last night."

"You were? About me?"

"No, no. About the big questions: Why we're here on Earth at just this time in history, what our purpose is, what one must do to be saved." He grins, blushes a little. "It was either that or a *Friends* rerun."

"I just meant at the animal shelter. Why am I at the animal shelter?"

"Oh, that I don't know."

He puts both hands deep into his pockets. She looks at the premonitory sky. He pretends to write something with the toe of his boot. Then says, "It's awkward times like these I always wish I smoked. If I had a fancy lighter we could talk about that. Or about my cigarette case, the silver one with my initials on it."

"Why don't you get one?"

"Oh, I'm not the cigarette case type. I bite my nails. Do you smoke?"

"Sara and I did. For a while." She watches a woman hurry past. She's sniffling. Her cardboard doggy-tote is empty.

"Could you French inhale?" Danny asks. "You know, where the smoke kind of leaks up out of your mouth and—"

"It's the first thing we did. I could show you if you want. I probably still remember."

He shakes his head. "I'd just cough. Why'd you guys stop?"

"My parents smoke, and I don't want to do anything those clowns do."

"'My parents smoke' makes me think of your folks kind of smoldering."

"My mother smolders. Or she thinks she does. Now, there's somebody whose idea of a big question is, 'What's on the Food Network?'"

A little girl exits the double doors of the pound. She clutches a puppy, brown with a white spot on its forehead.

"You picked a nice one," Danny tells her. "I know that one and he's a dandy."

Margaux watches the parents get into an SUV so large it looks like a condo on wheels. "It wouldn't matter if you were adopted, would it?" she says. "You could still get loathsome parents."

"*Loathsome*'s a little strong for these folks. Dad probably just wants a cocker spaniel for the Christmas card, but the mom looks nice. And the pooch will end up with her when the kid gets tired of it. She'll tell him her sorrows. When she cries, he'll lick the tears off her cheek. Then she'll buy them both an ice cream."

"You're such an odd guy."

"Compared to whom? One of the girls I work with bought herself a silver comb on eBay. She loves that comb. Got a piece of velvet to carry it in. Shows it to everybody every day. And Jose reads by moonlight."

"Why?"

Danny shrugs. "Makes the centerfold prettier maybe."

"He reads *Playboy* by moonlight?"

"As well as rival publications."

The diction pleases her. "And you hang out with these guys?"

"A little. Sometimes. We go out for pizza once a month or so."

"Are they nice?"

"Yeah. And durable."

She gives him a quizzical look.

"Dependable," he says. "Just basically right guys. But we do have one cad."

"Only one?"

"It's not really his fault. He's just really good-looking. Burdened with good looks, you might say."

"And that's the crew."

"And, oh, yeah, Laura. Who loves her nails. Does them perpetually."

"She doesn't get fired?"

"She's got kids. Mostly she answers the phones. She's okay."

"Danny!"

Margaux looks toward a side door. A stocky man in round sunglasses holds a screen open. "What about that chow with the scar?"

"They called, Luc. They're coming."

"Who's he?" she asks.

"Luc is from Vietnam." Danny gestures toward the screen-door side of the gray building with its inevitable red-tile roof. "Now, there's an interesting guy. He's the executioner."

"Oh, man."

"I want his job someday."

Margaux steps back. "Don't kid about stuff like that."

"Somebody has to do it. I can't yet. I get them back there where, you know, they have to go when nobody adopts them, and I just cry. It upsets the animals and makes things worse. But Luc is really good with them.

"He's not like Judas or anything. He doesn't betray them. He's just with them. You know what I mean? Right there with them. Not bored, not mean, not a big crybaby like somebody we know, not thinking about himself and how he'll die someday. None of that stuff. And afterward he doesn't rush in there with a shovel. He picks their bodies up one by one. I can do that part sometimes. But not the other."

Margaux puts her hand on his skinny arm. She wants to say something. Settles for, "He sounds amazing."

"Yes and no. He steals from everybody, too. From the lockers mostly."

"That doesn't make sense."

Danny grins. "Yeah, I know. That's why I like him so much."

When a car door slams, Danny looks that way. "These people own that chow Luc asked me about. I should go. Thanks for coming by. I'll see you later."

"What if you didn't?"

He doesn't look right at her. "Didn't see you?"

"Yeah, if we didn't, you know, talk or pet Blue or whatever. If we went back to not knowing each other."

"Are you thinking about doing that?"

"No."

"So it's a hypothetical question."

"Yes."

"Okay. Well, if that happened, that thing you said, if that happened I would figure it was because of me."

Margaux shakes her head. "It wouldn't be though. It'd be me. Being stupid or scared or something."

"I wouldn't know that."

"I'd tell you. I hope I would, anyway."

"It wouldn't matter. I'd still think it was me."

WHERE did you meet this one?" asks Margaux's mother, peering out the window.

"At AA."

"Why were you at AA? You're not an alcoholic."

"I went to get a map."

"That's Triple A. The auto club."

"Then why did they make me stand up and say my name?"

"What did you need a map for anyway?"

"I'm going out of my mind; I thought I'd take the scenic route."

"He's another one of Sara's friends, isn't he?"

"Yes."

"Why can't I get a straight answer from you anymore?"

"Sorry."

"No, you're not."

"No, I'm not."

They hear Margaux's date coming because at least two of the bolts have pulled loose, and the outside stairs rattle and sway like something in *Raiders of the Lost Ark.*

Her mother darts into the bedroom to change, so Margaux has to let the suitor in. The suitor. That's how she thinks of him. Maybe she'll go out with whomever Sara says to go out with, but she doesn't have to know their names.

Margaux opens the door. Sara was right; he is cute: a swimmer's body, tons of hair. His teeth are white as a king's pajamas. He's wearing cargo shorts, and there's a big sunburst tattoo on one calf.

"Welcome," she says. "We're just staying here while the villa is being worked on by Italian craftsmen."

He looks around: Margaux knows it's crummy — two bedrooms, one bath, a sink full of dishes all on a slant like tectonic, well, plates; framed pictures of horses on the wall.

"Who's this?" The suitor points to one of those.

"Uncle Bob."

"Seriously."

"That's his name. He's not my Uncle Bob. Otherwise my mother would be grazing instead of changing into something embarrassing. He was the last leg of a ninety-thousand-dollar Pick Six."

He looks puzzled.

"Forget it," Margaux says. "Racetrack lore."

He's chewing gum, chomping away. Then his grin widens slowly, like he's turning up a thermostat. He sidles closer. "I can't believe," he whispers, "I finally got you. My buddy's been after Sara forever to fix us up."

"What's that supposed to mean, 'I finally got you'?"

"Huh?"

"You said, 'I can't believe I finally got you.' What does that make me, the frightened doe and you the wily hunter? Are you going to rope me across the fender, tell the guys how you brought me down with one shot at four hundred yards, then mount my head on the wall?"

He's very glad to see Mom.

Hand out, he says his name, but not before Margaux puts her palms over her ears like there's a siren going by.

Mom has her lowest-slung jeans on and, to tread the terminal Earth (or, actually, the peat-brown carpet), little gold sandals. A silver ring on every toe but one. And there, a Band-Aid.

"Do you go to school at King?" she asks, clinging to his hand.

"No, ma'am. St. Luke's."

"Where your flesh," says Margaux, "turns to dust as soon as the air hits it."

Mom lays one hand on the suitor's forearm, leaves it there. "Don't pay any attention to her. She thinks she's so smart. You two have fun." She opens the scuffed front door. It has long scratch marks on it, like the inside of a coffin in a horror story.

They negotiate the precarious stairs. There's the pool with its oil slick, wine bottles on their sides, and the fake boulders someone got at a swap meet. The kids use them to play Buried Alive.

"Where's your dad?" asks Suitor.

"He's dead."

"No way. Sara said—"

"He just died. Like twenty minutes ago. When

I get home, Mom and I'll wash the body, then take him down to the ocean and push him out to sea on a flaming raft, because we're Vikings."

"Sara told me you were kind of thorny these days. Is it like, some girl thing?"

Margaux stops when she sees the Volvo with Sara and Somebody in the back seat. She beckons to her friend. Walks her away from the smirking boys.

"I can't do this, Sara."

"Why not? It's just another date."

"That's the point. It's the same date with the same hamburger at the same drive-in."

"Maybe we won't do that."

"Like it's better to stop by somebody's house for just a minute to pick up some CDs and then go in because his folks are gone and they wouldn't care, anyway?"

"I'm pretty sure they've got Jell-O shots in the fridge."

"I don't care."

"And some weed."

"I don't want that, either. And I really don't want somebody I barely know to stick his tongue down my throat while he tries to feel my boobs and I have to figure just the right moment to push him away so he'll think I'm just a semi-slut instead of a full-on hootchie."

Sara listens, shrugs, but says, "Suit yourself, but it sounds okay to me."

When Margaux comes into the apartment, her mother mutes both TVs. "What's wrong?"

"I'm sick at my stomach."

"What a shame. He was gorgeous."

"You go."

"Your father would kill me."

When the phone rings, Margaux seizes it. "What!"

"Is this a bad time?"

"Who is this?"

"Danny Riley."

"Oh."

"So is this a bad time?"

"Yes. No."

"Help me out a little. I've never been good at multiple choice."

"No, it's not a bad time."

"I was just going to, you know, make a run. And you said the next time I—"

"Don't move. I'll be right there."

Danny's sitting on the porch when she pulls up. Predictably, he hurries to meet her. Opens the car door. "I would've come by."

"That's okay. I had my keys in my hand."

"You're kind of dressed up."

She takes his hand, steps out of the car. "I stole these Ferragamos."

"What are Ferragamos?"

"Shoes." She models one for him, turning her ankle just so.

"Why did you steal them?"

"I don't know. Sara and I do stuff like that. Did. Stuff like that. Not anymore."

Danny heads for his car, already parked at the curb. "What is it about shoplifting, I wonder. It's irresistible."

"To you?"

"When I was eleven. Oh, yeah."

"What'd you steal?"

"Pens. From Staples. By the time Evie found my stash, I had about two hundred pens."

He starts the car, puts it in gear, and pulls away. She asks, "Then what?"

"Evie made me take them back. I had to tell the manager and promise not to do it again. She stood right there. Evie's tough. It was the right thing to do, though. I was pretty screwed up."

"Me, too, I guess. I'd stroll into Nordstrom's in beat-up flip-flops and out in some new Skechers."

"Why shoes?" he asks, making his eyebrows arc. "Was there somewhere you wanted to go?"

"Why pens? Was there something you wanted to write down?"

An old Toyota with a Domino's Pizza logo on the roof creeps past them going the other way, the driver searching for the right address.

Danny points. "When those guys come to our house, they say it's almost the only one with books. They can't believe it. According to them, all anybody in America does is watch TV. I show this one guy a Cavafy book and he has to try hard not to cry. Then he recites like twenty lines of "'Waiting for the Barbarians.'"

"Recite something for me."

"From Cavafy?"

"From anybody."

"Okay. Give me a second."

She likes it that he's choosing from some personal anthology. Some boy did murmur something metrical to her once. But it was one line. Something about a rose, of course.

"Okay." Danny points to a jacaranda tree. She can see the circle of fallen purple blossoms: beautiful debris.

"The trees are coming into leaf
Like something almost being said."

Danny's grin is huge. "I know it's not spring, but that's a killer opening, isn't it?"

"Who wrote that?"

"Philip Larkin. A Brit. Do you know his work? Evie loves him. I'll show you one of his books next time you're over."

He drives the speed limit. She leans back and breathes deeply. She likes a journey with no ulterior motives. No fast music, no one chuckling seismically at his own dumb jokes. No cloud of dark conceits.

Just a house with a roof red as the setting sun, a muscular man with a Weedwacker (his baseball hat is also red). In the dusk, two girls work intently on a hopscotch grid, leaning microscope-close, making it perfect. A man dressed as a Confederate soldier kisses his wife goodbye and goes off for a weekend of bloodless civil war. A couple of boys (one wearing his Halloween skeleton suit) throw a baseball in high arcs.

The street is level, but she feels like she's descending into Life or—if that capital is too pretentious—another life, then. A different one. Better. Better?

"How's Evie?"

He shrugs. "She was in bed at five-thirty. Evie is not a real good patient. She hates being sick."

"Doctors can't do anything?"

"Not really. She's tried alternative medicine: acupuncture, homeopathy, stuff like that. Sometimes it helps; sometimes it doesn't. She's got a stash of pills. I guess when it gets real bad, it's adios."

"Aren't you going to throw the pills away?"

"She'd just get more. Anyway, she doesn't know I know. And if she wanted me to know, she'd tell me."

"What'd she do before she got MS?"

"She was a lawyer. Still is, but mostly she just does pro bono work now. When she can. Six years ago, man, she was on the fast track: high-profile cases, lots of money. She wanted to be a partner before she was forty. Then she got sick."

"She's only in a wheelchair."

"Tell that to the firm of Scurrilous, Selfish, and Puke. They dropped her like a hot potato. And her boyfriend just freaked. First thing he said was, 'Can I catch it?'"

Margaux sits up straighter. "What'd she do?"

"Told the boyfriend to go to hell and sued the firm. They are really sorry they tried to do her wrong."

Danny glides to a stop in front of a modest two-story house, gray with white trim. Window boxes heavy with lobelia. Hose coiled politely like a snake in a cartoon. One green trash can with a rake—the toothy end—protruding.

Two dogs, matching setters but blond rather than red, gambol on a lawn littered with toys: kids' toys (red bucket, yellow shovel, Big Wheel, jump rope) and dog toys (a filthy stuffed sheep, balls of all sizes, huge rawhide chews like things on the floor of a cave or den).

"Oh, man, is that a pretty picture or not?"

Danny's arm slides along the back of the seat. He leans toward her. She knows he's not going to kiss her, or nuzzle her, or stick his tongue in her ear where it will explore like some dumb slug. And one hand will not creep disembodied across her shoulder, attach itself to one breast, and squeeze wildly. He just wants to get a better look at the dogs.

He's only inches away, his breath is sweet. He smells like powder. Baby powder.

"Ready to go?"

"In a minute," she replies.

So they watch the dogs tumble over each other, then play tug of war. Water from someone's sprinkler system gushes alongside the spotless curb. It turns in its leaf-strewn bed like a light sleeper.

Margaux's breathing deepens. Gets even. She can smell mint from somebody's garden. A possum waddles out from between some azaleas.

"Ever hear of Havahart traps?" Danny asks.

"I can imagine."

"Yeah. Catches them without hurting them. Then somebody brings 'em to us, and we take them down to the arroyo and let them go."

"Then what?"

Danny grins. "They hike back up here for the gourmet garbage."

"Speaking of fine dining, could we get something to eat? Pastoral scenes always give me an appetite."

She likes to make him smile, though it's still him smiling: weak-chinned, thin-lipped, slope-shouldered him.

There's a retro drive-in twenty or so blocks away, a drive-in with waitresses on roller skates and little trays like diving platforms for Chihuahuas. They go there.

She's been to Hot Wheels before with boys in better cars. Much, much better cars. And what was she then except a bauble, really? A flunky with killer legs. Macaroni: a feather in their caps.

And what was she now? Hungry.

They order stuff you're supposed to order when you're in high school: cheeseburgers, fries, chocolate malts. She likes it that he doesn't talk much/doesn't have to talk/doesn't feel compelled. She watches him watch the girls on skates without a flicker of desire. He might be interested in nothing but balance and velocity.

When the food comes, he passes her things, then frowns.

"I, uh, don't know how to say this exactly."

"What?" Has she done something wrong? Been something wrong?

"I sort of pray before I eat. I know, I know. It's ridiculous."

"No." She gestures with her cheeseburger. "It's nice. It's fine. Who do you pray to?"

"I don't know exactly." He picks up a French fry. Puts it down. Doesn't meet her eyes. "God, I guess. Buddha, maybe. The Creative Influx. I'm really not sure."

"It's fine, Danny. Go ahead."

"I do it, you know, silently."

"Okay."

"Well, I can't now. I'm not used to being with a girl."

"Should I talk in a deep voice about the NFL?"

"Actually I'm not used to being anywhere with anybody."

"Do you want me to just shut up?"

"It's okay. I just did it really fast. To myself."

"When?"

"Like a second ago."

"What did you say?"

"That I'm grateful."

"To . . . ?"

"To just, you know, everything that died so I could eat dinner."

"Like the pickle?"

There's that weightless smile. "You're kind of fun to be with, you know that? Word on the street is that you're frivolous and cruel."

"Is that what you think?"

"No way. I'm having a good time. If this is a date, and I'm not saying it is, this is the best one I was ever on. But, then, it's pretty much the only one I was ever on."

That makes her collect herself. "You're kidding."

"Can you really see me dating?"

"I'd have to squint."

"Right. That's why I only have friends."

"Like me."

"And some others, yeah."

Margaux scoots closer. "For instance."

"Well, besides the crew at the pound, there's a couple of kids at school."

"They come to the house?"

"Not exactly."

"They know Evie?"

"Not personally."

"So I'm the friend. The Lone Friend."

"Maybe I'm practicing with you for when I get a real one."

"Oh." She covers her heart with both hands, pretends to be wounded.

"I had to start with small animals," he explains.

"Puppies?"

"Not even puppies. They were too much for me at first. All that jumping around and slobbering. Too much unconditional love, as my therapist used to say. But there was this turtle."

"From the pound?"

"Well, yeah, from the pound. What'd you think? From some weird classified ad: 'Lonely tortoise wants to meet relationship-challenged human for long slow walks?"

"So there you are at the pound with your first friend."

"I was the only one who could pet him, you

know, who he'd leave his head out for. And he'd eat for me, lettuce and stuff, when nobody else could feed him."

Margaux looks at her right hand. It's steady. "And made bold by your success . . ."

"Exactly. I did kittens, then puppies, and finally I graduated to grown-up dogs. Took me a long time."

"And now me."

"You know my stock's gone way up lately. Guys at school who never talked to me say hi. In gym, they ask me what you're like."

"Those creeps."

"Not all of them. There's some girls, too. Who are curious. Two or three, anyway. You're kind of an enigma, Margaux. Everybody knows there's more to you than just that act you and Sara put on."

"So what do you tell 'em?"

"That you're nice. That you're interesting."

"Hey!"

She glances up. It's Wesley Powers peering in the window.

"Are you comin' to the game, Margaux?"

"Maybe."

"Come to the game."

"Maybe."

"It's gonna be a good game."

"We'll see."

He pounds the top of the car with the mallet of his palm. "Cool. See you at the game."

When he's gone, Margaux says, "He should write sestinas. He only knows six words, anyway."

Danny nods. "It makes you think biology is destiny, doesn't it? What else is a big guy like Wes going to do but play ball. And then there's his name: Powers. He didn't stand a chance. Of course that makes me Danny Riley, wistful tenor."

Margaux shakes her head. "I don't know about biology and destiny. I think it's what happens to you that really matters."

Danny takes a discrete spoonful of malt. "You believe in the tabula rasa then. That when we're born, we're like blank pieces of paper, then we get written on and that story is who we are?"

"Maybe. Especially if somebody writes disgusting stuff."

She can feel him shy away from that. Not like a thoroughbred, all rolling eyes and hooves in the air. More like a delicate sea creature that retreats when the temperature changes one degree.

Any other boy would want to know everything. Then any other boy would be outraged. Outraged and full of compassion. Full of prurient compassion: "Really? Your dad did that? Are you kidding? Have you got any Polaroids?"

Just then the entire car starts to rock. At first Margaux thinks it's an earthquake. Like a good California teenager, the first thing she does is grab her malt so it won't spill. Then she glances in the rearview mirror and sees somebody, a big somebody, riding the back bumper. Bouncing on it.

"Another friend of yours?" asks Danny.

"Former."

A head covered with black hair except for a plume of white in front comes through the window on Margaux's side. It sings, "Oh, Danny boy!"

"Cut it out, Noah. This isn't funny."

Noah looks at Margaux. "You shut up."

Danny chews, swallows, politely wipes his mouth with a napkin. "What can I do for you, Noah?"

"I just want to warn you about something, man. This one's going to get you going, then leave you high and dry."

"Okay."

"I mean it, man."

Danny nods. "I understand."

"She's a teasing bitch, dude."

Danny sighs, says to Margaux, "I have to get out now and defend your honor."

"No, you don't."

"Yeah, I do."

She grips his thin wrist. "God, why? I'm not very honorable."

"Sure you are. Besides, I don't want to come back to my fiftieth class reunion and have some guy with a pacemaker croak, 'Remember when you punked out at Hot Wheels?'" He pats her hand. "I'll be right back. And I mean that. This won't take long."

He opens the door, exits. "Noah! Come around to this side, please. I'd rather fall down over here. The concrete looks softer."

Noah's fast, and he makes this neat little stuntman move where he pretty much vaults across the hood. He lands just a bit off balance, though, so Danny launches himself at him and they go down together.

A carhop screams and drops a tray of root beer. The fat security guard hurries toward the ruckus, which is over in less than a minute. Everybody involved is eighty-sixed after a stern and rather Biblical leave-this-garden-never-to-return-again lecture.

Minutes later they're parked on a side street not far from the wrangle and grease of Hot Wheels. Danny presses a handkerchief to his face.

Margaux leans. "You okay?"

"I always wanted a new nose. Now I've got one."

"Thanks for standing up for me."

"From what I hear guys fight over you all the time."

"But it's always totally about them. How strong they are. Or to make all their karate lessons pay off."

He says, "I need to join a gym. It was like he didn't even feel it when I punched him."

Margaux has one hand on his shoulder. "You could go with me. I go a lot."

"Obviously. You look great." He glances at the handkerchief, frowns. "Let's see. If I worked out three times a week for six years, I'd be half as strong as Noah. I wonder if that's really a good use of my time."

"You know, actually I was kind of a tease." She rubs his arm absently. Her fingers disappear into a tear in his shirt and stay there. Against his skin. "Sara and I were. Are. She is. Still. Probably."

"Why?"

"Why is she?"

"No, why were you?"

"It was Sara's idea and I went along with it. She was the closest thing I had to a friend." She tugs his hand away from his face. Checks things out. "You're not bleeding anymore."

"If there's one thing I'm good at, it's coagulating." He stuffs the handkerchief in his pocket, feels one shoulder (the left), and winces. He tugs at his sleeve, finds a rip. "Gee, my beautiful shirt."

"Which you found . . . ?"

"You don't want to know."

"Do you make rags out of these when they're really, really old?"

"How'd you guess?"

"I can just see you with your official Save the Planet scissors." She's not being mean. She's closer to him, nearly whispering.

Danny rolls down the window. The way the light slants, Margaux can see only half his face. "I can't," he says, "stand to see anything neglected or, you know, mistreated. Even a pair of pants. I think it's because my dad beat the crap out of me when I was little. But Evie says I was probably a mean, indifferent bastard in a former life and I'm paying off my karmic debt."

Now she moves closer, slips under his right arm, slides hers across his chest. She hears his heart surge and whoosh.

He pats her. Pets her hair. It's rough and tumble enough that she half expects him to throw a stick.

"If this was a movie," he says, "we'd make out now because I told you my dark secret. But first of all, I wouldn't be any good at it. When I was ten, a girl at a party said I was the worst kisser in the world and that included Trinidad and Tobago."

"So," Margaux asks into his shirt, "what's second of all?"

"I don't think my plans include stuff like that."

"What plans are those?"

"Uh, well, I'm not exactly sure. Evie says I just need to be patient. The Quakers call it waiting for the way."

She breathes when he does, likes how they rise and fall together. "Do those Quakers quake while they wait?"

She feels him laugh. Chuckle, actually. "You

know, when Evie and I talk about stuff like this, it sounds okay. When I tell you, the words kind of get unstuck from what I thought they meant."

"Don't pay any attention to me," says Margaux. "I was raised by louts. And don't worry about kissing. Sara says, 'Most of the time it's like going to the dentist: unpleasant but necessary.'"

Danny grins. "Saint Thomas said if kissing is fun, it's a mortal sin."

"How do you know such weird stuff?"

"It's Evie's fault. She reads all the time and then tells me." He squirms, sits up straighter. "Last night I get this: if you love someone, you accept him as he is. But if you accept him as he is, you don't really love him, because if you did, you'd want the best for him and that usually means he needs to be better than he is." He looks at Margaux and crosses his eyes.

"Evie told you this over dinner."

"After. No wonder I had a stomachache."

"She's talking about you. She loves you, and she wants you to be better than you already are."

"Maybe. But remember at the end of *Fahrenheit*

451 how everybody had memorized a book? Evie's starting to forget stuff. So I'm her book, sort of. A walking reference library. Why is that love? Why isn't it just self-interest?"

"All my parents ever talk about is what was on TV or how much my dad won."

A car buzzes by. There's a siren in the distance. A bird lands on the hood, then lifts off. It's quiet on the plum-dark street. Light falls on the black macadam, making circles like enormous snares.

"We could hold hands if you wanted," Danny says. "Except I don't even know who goes first."

"We'll do it together," she says. "On three. Three."

"Very funny. Listen, do you need to call your folks? It's getting late."

"They're not like that."

He nods. "Well, we're on our way home, anyhow."

Home. What a joke. It's just an apartment.

She tries it out loud: "Apartment, sweet apartment."

He gets it, adds one of his own. "There's no place like apartment."

"The land of the free," she says, "and the apartment of the brave."

"Oh, give me an apartment, where the buffalo roam." He's laughing and tugging gently at her. "I can't start the car until you give my hand back. How am I doing, anyway?"

"At holding hands? Very good. Not too much pressure. No excess perspiration. High marks all around. A ten from the German judge."

"You're very good, too."

"I thought this was your first time."

"Well, yeah, but I've done considerable research."

"Meet me for lunch tomorrow."

"Really?" He starts the car. "You'd eat lunch with me at school?"

Margaux's English teacher, Ms. Honeybee, assigns a poem, then stands by the window. The poem is good, rich but not fattening. Margaux finishes first, reads it again, holds a noun or two under her tongue like a homeopathic remedy. Then she watches her teacher, who has posed by the window to gaze at her engagement ring. It starts to rain on cue. Ms. Honeybee (so named for her teaching voice, a low-pitched, soporific buzzzz) pushes back a lock of hair. Adjusts the cameo at her neck (incongruous above her Serengeti safari vest, the cartridge loops empty except for the one with lipstick). She sighs. She might be looking out over a moor instead of a parking lot. Her lover gallops toward her on a lathered steed. He is intact, except for a single, blindingly white bandage on his deeply tanned cheek.

What a sap. Maybe Danny is right and romance is for the birds.

An hour later, Margaux listens to Sara and a couple of her dunderhead acolytes describe some farcical gymnastics in the inevitable back seat.

Has she done that? She has done that. Both done it and talked about it. She's no better than these two chatterboxes, one of whom wears a zucchini-green thong, part of which shows above her low-slung jeans. On purpose. It makes Margaux want to wear a duffle bag so that not even her head shows.

Then Danny appears. Spies her. Hesitates—this is the heartbreaker—because she's talking to her pals. He doesn't want to intrude.

So she goes to him.

"I didn't want to intrude." He might have read her mind.

"Believe me, it was nothing special. Are you hungry?"

"I just need to go by the office; then I'll meet you."

So she waits at the cafeteria's big double doors. (Has she waited for a boy before? Ever?) Tells Sara to go on. She nods to a few people. The tenth-graders eye her, then each other, then they whisper: a meadowy susurration that she used to pretend to like. But not anymore.

She's entertaining that thought (which means what—pouring it a drink? Bringing it a snack?) when Danny appears, startling her. It's like he approached on slippered feet. Or in moccasins like every savage in the novels of James Fenimore Cooper. Which she has read. On her own, no less. When she was nine.

She blurts, "If my friends are stupid, am I stupid?"

He shrugs. "Don't ask me. I still think if all men are mortal and Aristotle is a man, then all men are Aristotle."

"That would explain the sudden popularity of togas."

They laugh together, something else she's never done with a guy. And whose fault was that? Were they all jerks all the time? Or was at least one of them nice and she was just too petty, too fond of her own wounds, too addicted to polysyllables to see?

He points to the open door. "After you."

She's glad he's polite, and glad he's not cute. She's sick of cute. She's tired of cheekbones as sharp as car parts and of guys who can't think of anything but their hair, some of it so gelled and moussed it looks like something from a tide pool.

He hands her a brown, frayed-at-the-edges cafeteria tray, and they get in line.

She peers, then turns. "It looks like today's special is hoof."

"I think that's stuffed pepper."

A cafeteria lady in a hairnet, wielding a fork as big as Neptune's trident, spears one, passes it over the hot stainless steel.

He tries to pay, but she won't let him. She pays for his, in fact, because "I asked you." He's grateful without licking her shoe.

The cafeteria rumbles with insults and hip-hop. A guy who must do a thousand sit-ups a day walks around in half a football jersey. Someone else is doing prep-school boy: blazer, loose tie, rumpled chinos, Converse high-tops. A sigh here, ululation there. Sensorium meets nobody home. Eloquence, say hello to dysphonia.

"Where do you want to sit?" he asks.

"With the Metaphysical poets."

"Gee, all those seats are taken."

She likes it that he doesn't say, "Huh?" She's sick of *huh,* too, that interjection of ignorance.

Once settled (he held her chair, of course), he straightens his tray. Then hers. Getting the edges squared. His baked apple is even with his milk carton. He reunites the estranged salt and pepper shakers until it's them against the world.

He picks up a spoon, wipes it clean/cleaner with a napkin, and asks, "Is this the one that ran away with the dish?"

Margaux nods. "Now, there's an odd relationship."

"Yeah, I wonder if that worked out, or did they end up on *Jerry Springer*?"

Then he begins to eat. He holds the fork tines down, like someone on *Masterpiece Theatre.* Who taught him that—Evelyn? Or did he just see it somewhere and decide to adopt it? Be that way. Be that person. Even if the fork is plastic and the knife (now in his other hand) dull as an album cover.

When a cafeteria worker walks by with a flat, cardboard turkey and a thumbtack, Danny asks, "What do you do for the holidays?"

"Dad goes to the track; then he brings home a turkey dinner from Denny's."

"There's racing on Thanksgiving?"

"That's what he's thankful for."

"Do you have relatives in L.A.? Aunts, uncles, that kind of thing?"

"None of those around. What do you guys do?"

"Before Evie got sick, hotshots from the office would come by."

"And now?"

"It's turned into an orphan's caucus: single parents, F1 visa clients who don't know anybody, people from the waiting room at her doctor's office. That kind of thing. It's total chaos. We cook for like two days ahead of time."

"Do you ever see your dad?"

"He's history." He looks at his hands. Sighs. Rallies. "Listen, speaking of eating, do you want to come to dinner sometime? Evie'd like that."

"Sure. When?"

"Saturday? Or is Saturday bad?" He doesn't look at her. "You're probably always busy on Saturday."

"Saturday's fine."

"Cool. I'll pick you up at six."

"I don't mind driving over. I know where you—"

"No, I should come by. I'm the boy."

"Hey, kids."

It's Sara. Her short, red hair is swept back; her T-shirt says ZOOM.

When Danny stands up, Margaux says, "He's not leaving; he's just being polite." Then she begins, "Danny, this is—"

"Everybody knows Sara."

Margaux remembers that's pretty much what he said to her: "Everybody knows you." And she gets this little pang of, what—jealousy? But why? Everybody does know Sara. That's the point. That was their point, hers and Sara's—to be known by everybody. To be famous. Or infamous.

This time he holds Sara's chair.

"I can only stay a minute," she says. "The governess has the twins and I'm dining with the duke."

Margaux warns her, "Don't be a snot."

He stays on his feet. "I'm going to get some ice cream to keep that baked apple company. Anybody want anything?"

Sara lets him get ten feet away before she leans forward.

"What's up with you? First you won't go out with Chet, and two hours later you show up at Hot Wheels with Raggedy Andy, who gets in a fight with Noah?" She takes Margaux's hand. "People are talking."

"About Danny and me?"

"Yes, about Danny and you. I'm jealous. I wonder if he'd go out with me. Is he a good kisser?"

"He doesn't do stuff like that. We just hold hands."

"No kidding. And then what—you fetch a pail of water?"

GETTING DRESSED Saturday night, she thinks about what Danny said: "I'm the boy." And likes it, because it makes her the girl. Not the school beauty, not a naughty minx like Sara. Just the girl.

Looking through her underwear, she finds nothing that isn't designed to please, to instigate, to give her the upper hand. Yet is, still and always, servile. And it's not like he's going to see them. Nobody has ever seen her that undressed. Almost nobody.

She still chooses the least reproachful, decides on some khakis she actually paid for, and a light, cornflower-blue sweater.

Will Danny even notice? Evie will, so she'll dress for Evie. Who'll like her better then. Maybe. Trust her, even. (Though Margaux doesn't trust anybody except, maybe, now, a little, Danny.)

Her mother appears in the open bedroom door. She's wearing a blue exercise outfit (matching pants and top with bolts of white lightning down each leg) and she's smoking.

"Is this another one of Sara's friends?"

"No, one of mine."

"Really?" She taps ashes into one cupped palm. "Since when do you have friends of your own?"

* * *

That night, Danny is as presentable as she's ever seen him: jeans, polo shirt, loafers. And everything fits. More or less.

"So you go to school with my daughter?" Margaux's mother asks.

"Yes, ma'am. And I work for the Humane Society part-time."

Mom sidles to the window. Peers out. "Which car is yours?"

"You probably can't see it from here. It tends to disappear." He glances at Margaux. "In the gloaming."

She is loving this. Of course, the unusual noun like an hors d'oeuvre, but mostly the way her mother keeps looking at her like there's been some mistake. Like Danny belongs next door where the lumpy girl lives. Or like he'll soon begin to try to sell her a vacuum cleaner or set of encyclopedias.

Danny takes a folded piece of paper out of one pocket. Passes it to Margaux's mom. "We're going to have dinner at my aunt's house. Here's the number, just in case."

She just stares at it. She never knows where her daughter is.

Danny extends one hand. "A pleasure to meet you."

"Likewise." Mom rallies, turning Danny's hand over, caressing his palm, putting the make on him like she does with all the others. "You have sensitive fingers. Do you play an instrument or sculpt?"

"Gee, no. I just clean the dog runs."

"Oh." She wipes her hands on her jeans.

Walking to the car, Margaux holds on to him. Grips his left arm with both hands. He's so skinny, it's like clinging to a rope, so different from the biceps of the usual date, the biceps he evaluates in his full-length mirror ten times a day.

"You look nice," she says.

"I went to the thrift store. I needed some . . ."

"New old clothes?"

"Yeah."

When Danny opens the car door for her, she turns.

She wants to kiss him, but just in some neutral

way. Some agape-not-eros way. Like disciples kiss. Or brave French freedom fighters. Or like the lost hiker kisses the cold cheeks of the rescue party.

"Okay if I give you a hug?"

"Sure. I guess."

"I'm not going too fast for you, am I?"

"I don't know."

She touches him here and there: cheek, shoulder, clavicle. But lightly, like he's a confection made of spun sugar. When she puts both arms around him, he's sealed tight as a time capsule. He keeps his arms at his sides.

Minutes later, Margaux is not surprised to see the house suffused with light, all from candles, all but a few of those in hurricane lamps with shapely chimneys.

Evelyn waits at the front door, completely in white, including some kind of slipper socks.

"Sober this time," she says as Margaux climbs the stairs. "But my damn head won't sit up straight; I look like a mum that needs water."

Her face is flushed, and a few strands of hair

cling to her broad forehead, while the proffered hand is hot and dry. Margaux has an odd series of thoughts: like photos in an album. Or like tarot cards capsized to reveal scenes both common and mysterious: Evelyn weaker and thinner; Danny skulking in the dark; her mother as an older woman peering out a smeared window; her father, seedy and disheveled, in front of an enormous slot machine. And her? Where is she?

Inside, Evelyn says, "Let's have something cool to drink." Margaux settles onto a brown leather couch. The glasses Danny brings are turquoise.

"Sun tea," he says, bowing slightly. As he retreats, Margaux notices he has taken off his shoes. Both socks are thin at the heel.

When the swinging door closes, Evelyn begins, "I didn't mean to be rude last time. I'd just come from the doctor, and—"

"Danny told me."

"And I'd had a few drinks, so—"

"It's okay. Really."

"No hard feelings." Out comes that fervid

hand again. Which Margaux takes, and Evelyn doesn't let go. "What size are you?"

"Five."

"You might want to look anyway."

"Look at what?"

"Oh, my closet. I'm starting to give things away. There's a really lovely camelhair coat. It'd need altering, but it'd be worth it. I don't know what I'm going to do with my underwear. I have drawers of beautiful underwear. I used to prance around for my boyfriend." She tries to lift her cheek off her shoulder and fails. "But since the house burned down, there's been a lot less prancing."

Margaux looks at the solid walls, quicksilver windows, the urns, the curtains that seem to breathe on their own.

"Not that house," Evie says, pointing to herself. Her body. "This one."

Margaux notices a heedlessness in Evelyn tonight, and she remembers her English teacher's stories of tubercular poets — how smitten and rash they became.

Evelyn struggles to lift her head again. "I saw a psychic once who said this isn't the lifetime for marriage or for career. At least not the kind I planned. So now I do a lot of pro bono work." A glance to make sure.

"I know what *pro bono* means." No edge, just reassurance.

"Of course you do. I'm sorry. Anyway, I do a lot of that and people I helped two or three or five years ago still send me cards that say THANK YOU. Or if they don't speak English, the card might say HAPPY SEVENTEENTH BIRTHDAY. When I was well, I worked fourteen hours a day and nobody liked me."

"If your clients didn't speak English," Margaux asks, "how did you help them?"

"Oh, I speak a lot of Spanish and a little Mandarin."

Danny pushes open the hinged kitchen door, says, "Won't be long now," lets it swing shut. Opens it again, "You okay, Margaux?"

"I'm fine, Danny."

Once they're alone, Evelyn's eyes narrow. "I can't figure you two out."

"Me neither."

Now Evie juts forward in her wheelchair. She looks streamlined and fierce, like the figurehead of a ship named *The Lion of God.* She rasps, "If you hurt him, somebody in a dark suit will show up at your door."

"I understand."

"You actually like him."

"I like being with him."

"God, so do I." She retreats, sinks almost. "When I got sick, Danny and I spent hours trying to figure things out. We read everything: Christian Science, karma/dharma, guilt and retribution, past lives, you name it. I saw clairvoyants, went to Rolfers, meditated. If I was just supposed to be a nicer person, I thought, 'Okay, now I am. So I can get out of this chair and be nice on my feet.' Didn't happen. Is this too much information all at one time?"

"No. It's a whole lot better than listening to some fathead talk about how many points the Lakers scored."

"Do you know about Danny's father?"

"He told me a little. What happened to his

mom? Where was she when he was getting beat up?"

"Dead. Died of a heart attack at thirty-three. It crushed the father. They were churchgoers. Straight arrows. But after Nancy died, Walter just went to pieces. Took most of it out on Danny. When I finally got custody of him, he couldn't even talk. For the first six months, I just held him."

"I didn't get a lot of that. My dad was playing cards and my mom had a remote in each hand."

"Danny says your father is a professional gambler."

"Yes."

"Can he support a family?"

"He's pretty good at it. Most of the time."

"And when he's not?"

"He, uh, takes the necessary steps."

Evelyn grimaces. "That sounds sinister."

"It was. I hate him."

"Well, according to the Torah, you should . . ." Evelyn frowns, furrows her brow. "Damn it! Danny! What does the Torah say about hatred? We were just talking about it."

He answers from the kitchen. "Uh, 'Do not hate your brother in your heart,' and then something about offering guidance and assistance."

"Right, right. 'Rebuke him' is in there, and then the guidance and assistance bit."

"I should rebuke my dad?"

"If he's done something wrong? Absolutely."

Danny enters carrying a black lacquered tray, lifts three matching blue plates, and sets those out, then backs toward the kitchen. "Why don't you guys come on? I'll get the bread and the kebabs."

Evelyn rolls toward the empty table. Her chair — not the wheelchair but the real chair — sits in the corner, turned rather ominously toward the wall like it's being punished.

She slides a blue napkin out of its silver ring, then smiles at the table, adjusts a candle, fusses — tries to fuss — with a bazaar trivet. She cautions, "Sit somewhere you don't have to watch me miss my mouth. It isn't pretty."

"Don't pay any attention to Evie," Danny says from the doorway. "She thinks her only choices are preemptive strikes or whining."

"I," Evelyn says, "don't whine, and I have no intention of going gentle into that or any other good night."

He moves the meat, still impaled by bamboo skewers, closer to his aunt. "This is just from some little restaurant Evie likes. I didn't cook it or anything."

Evelyn sounds alarmed. "I hope you're not vegetarian, Margaux." Then she laughs. "Now there's a model sentence for you: same cadence as 'I hope you're not a bride of the undead.'"

"I'm not a vegetarian," Margaux says, "and I admit I used to date the undead, but we never got serious."

Danny grins as he reaches for his aunt's hand. "We're going to pray, Margaux. You don't have to do anything."

Margaux bows her head, listens to Danny say, "Bless this food to the nourishment of our bodies. Make us available to those things that are for our highest good."

She waits for what happens next. Accepts one plate, passes another. Danny and Evelyn start to eat.

Nobody says anything. It's like a little monastery. Or nunnery, maybe.

When they're finished, Danny clears the table.

"We usually read after dinner," Evie says.

Margaux is startled to hear a voice after so much silence.

Evelyn nods toward the bookshelves. "Take your pick. And since you're the guest, you get the couch."

"Should we wait for Danny?"

"He'll be in shortly. Reading soothes him." She sounds like she's talking about something big and unreliable that needs to hear a beautiful harpist or a virgin who sings.

So Margaux finds a book of poems that looks interesting. Danny does return, sits, reaches for a book. Even in his clean clothes that almost fit, crumpled in that chair he still looks like litter.

"Margaux, give me a hand here."

Bossy Evelyn wants to deliver light, so Margaux pushes while Evelyn, with one cupped hand, guards the flame.

"Honey, here's your favorite candle."

"Oh, great, Evie." Danny glances up at Margaux. "Now everybody at school will know I've got a favorite candle."

Margaux reassures him, "Your secret's safe with me."

Evelyn propels herself backward, finds a pair of half-glasses, takes her own volume off a low shelf, opens it, and leans forward.

Margaux returns to the couch. Candlelight plays across Evelyn's face. On her lap lies the open book, and inside that, someone rain-soaked coughs and puts one hand to his tender chest.

Danny reads. Once he stops breathing, leans forward and turns two or three pages rapidly. Then color returns to his cheeks. He has all but disappeared into the story.

Margaux dips in and out of her book like someone beside a stream. That the black marks on the paper mean the same thing to millions of people comforts her like a cool hand on her brow. It's funny. She'll tell Sara anything that any boy says or does or tries to do. But she would never tell

Sara that she likes to read. Does read. Likes school (most of it). Is proud of her good grades.

Then turning to a poem about a robot mother, she can't help but think of her own. Her human mother. Who taught her to read with catalogs. "Jewelry," she said, underlining the word with a scarlet talon. Then she pointed to the bracelet on some model's perfect wrist. "Sale." At that point they'd switch from reading to math—what it used to cost, what it costs now, how much she saved.

Or Margaux would stand beside her father and read out loud the names of racehorses—Palomino Poco, Midnight Snow, Cottage in the Pines. *Do it for me, sweetheart. I'm in big trouble. And don't tell your mom. It's our secret, okay?*

Oh, God, not those grim archives.

With a shudder, she wrests herself into the present. Watches Danny reach for another book. Thinner than the one in his lap. Watches him write something, moving his lips as he copies.

Evelyn speaks up. "It's his vade mecum." She says it offhandedly enough, but Margaux detects the snob Evelyn once was. The know-it-all go-getter. Gal on the way up. Until she was brought low.

She looks at Danny's aunt. On the table beside her stands a wooden bowl of walnuts and half a glass of wine, red as stallion's blood. A still life.

Danny stretches. "It just means a little book you carry around with you. And I don't even do that." He holds it up like an auctioneer. "This guy never leaves the house."

"Can I see it?"

He looks at her, then hands it over. She peers in.

Love in action is a harsh and dreadful
thing compared to love in dreams.

—Feodor Dostoyevsky

Although you never wanted, did you,
a journey as simple as that?

—Elizabeth Spires

For I the Lord thy God am a jealous God,
visiting the iniquity of the fathers upon
the children.

—Exodus 20:5

"It's just stuff that I thought was interesting. It's not, you know, a Rorschach. It's not like somebody could read this and figure me out."

Really? But that's a question Margaux keeps to herself.

"Would you like a journal?" Evelyn asks, rolling toward a tall cupboard against the west wall. "Come."

Shadowy blue veins show at Evelyn's neck and wrists. A pulse at her throat throbs. She beckons like someone in a novel involving a secret garden.

When Margaux is close enough, Evelyn throws open the doors of the distressed, worn-out-on-purpose blue cabinet. There they are: on one shelf stacked neatly like volumes ready for shipping, yet sprawled on the second tier as if some child had been playing with them, building mute towers that he could topple onto the lairs of animal-faced supermen.

She imagines Danny playing here as a child, safe from his furious, bereaved father.

"Evie's into memoranda," says Danny.

"Maybe there's stuff I want to remember, smarty-pants."

Margaux takes in all the diaries/journals/notebooks: some smaller than a palm, some large as the screen on a confessional. Soft cover and hard, spiral and perfect bound, stapled and sewn. Pristine, untouched, virginal. Silver like a spaceman's shoes. Vehemently blue. Fiercely yellow. A thin pink, a rusty brown like the empty drums homeless people build fires in. One with a mirror on the front, another in white leather like a good girl's Bible. Hello Kitty on a third. A racecar here, a picture of scissors there. A Virgin Mary. A woman in a sari leering at a steak.

Evelyn holds one out. "This feels like you, kid. Just because you're gorgeous doesn't mean things have been easy. You might want to write about that sometime."

Then they read again. For what seems like hours. Margaux turns one languid page after another. The fragmented words float up at her like the letters in Campbell's alphabet soup, her mother's idea of a nutritious meal.

* * *

"Margaux." Danny whispers it. "Help me get Evie to bed. Do you mind?"

"God, I dozed off."

"You push her, okay? I'll get the doors."

Evelyn's bedroom is very well appointed: lush carpet pale as martyrs' feet, platform bed with a deep scarlet comforter. A computer with a tiny base like an igloo and a large screen takes up most of a well-organized desk. One wall is decorated with silver stirrups and a bridle, all inlaid with turquoise. On another hangs a picture of a man in a loincloth in the middle of an ocean; he's balanced on a tiny strip of bamboo.

"Who's that?" Margaux asks as Danny turns the comforter back to reveal mustard-colored sheets.

He answers without looking up. "Bodhidharma. The guy who brought Zen Buddhism to China. He sort of surfed there, or at least that's how the story goes."

"So are you guys Buddhists?"

"Not exactly."

"What are you then?"

"Just curious, I guess. About how things work. Why things turn out the way they do."

"When you were in the kitchen, Evelyn told me how much you guys read, trying to figure stuff out."

"Yeah, every night. We were looking for a congenial belief system."

"So did you find one?"

A shrug. "I'm not sure, but it's more fun to believe in something instead of nothing." He smoothes his aunt's hair. "Evie. Wake up. It's time to go to bed. Do you need to pee?"

Evelyn stirs, tries to look up, squints instead. "Some Saturday night for you, huh, Margaux? I hope the thrill isn't too much."

"Can you take her left side?" Danny asks.

Evelyn is heavy. Heavier than Margaux would have guessed. She shuffles as Danny revolves. Evelyn sits on the bed with a grunt. Reaches for Margaux's hand. "Come back soon. We'll light all the candles and let Danny wait on us again. Maybe I'll pitch forward into the guacamole."

Margaux takes one tropical hand. "I'll bring the chips."

Danny asks, "You want pajamas?"

"No, sweetie. I'll sleep in this outfit. I already drooled on it." She falls back, speaks straight up in the air. "You guys can go out now. I'll be fine here by myself. Transylvania has beautiful nights. I'll just open the window and slip out of this cumbersome crucifix."

Danny leans over her. "Need anything else?"

"A new body."

"If we go by the mall, I'll see what I can do."

She seizes his wrist. Really seizes it. "What was the name of that book they used in the Inquisition to torture all those women?"

"The Devil's Hammer. Malleus Maleficarum."

"I knew that yesterday."

"Latin's hard to remember."

"And English. And Mandarin. But not Spanish. Why is that?"

"Is she going to be all right by herself?"

"She doesn't want somebody hovering over her all the time," Danny says. "It makes her feel like a sick person."

Standing in the driveway, Margaux turns. The house is dark except, she knows, for night-lights, each delicate and expensive: a butterfly with purple wings, a thatched cottage, a sprite with fiery hair.

"You looked like Sleeping Beauty in there," says Danny.

And where is he in that story? Margaux wonders. *Outside holding the prince's horse? Sweeping the kitchen with a magic broom?*

"Some Sleeping Beauty I am. I usually have to take these pills Sara gets."

He nods sympathetically. "I'm awake about half the night myself."

"What do you do then, meditate or something?"

"I should, but I'm really bad at it. All I do is think about the dogs. Evie's a great meditator."

"I don't know what I'd do if I was like that, in a wheelchair and everything."

"Man, me neither. But she just keeps saying, 'Lord, don't let me miss the lesson in all this.'"

He turns the engine over; the idle is perfect.

Danny angles his face away, pretends to listen harder to the engine. Blurts, "Evie made me take a class so I can work on my own car. She taught me to cook a little. I can sew on a button. I know a growth fund from a bond fund. She doesn't want me to be helpless when she, you know—"

"She isn't really going to die anytime soon, is she?"

Danny shrugs. "Probably not. Nobody knows. But I'm not going away to college. No way am I leaving her. I wouldn't even be here if it wasn't for her. What about you? Can't you go to just about anyplace you want next year?"

"With a scholarship maybe."

"So apply. Have you applied?"

"Not yet."

As he drives, she watches the chaste, moon-bleached houses. Outside one, a child in a cowboy suit practices with a six-gun. He draws across his body—right hand reaching for the other revolver, holstered backward. He'd seen it on TV, in an old movie. He thought it was cool. Unique.

He wanted to be that man. If only until he had to go to bed.

She asks, "Do you go to the movies?"

"Videos mostly. Stuff Evie wants to see."

"TV?"

"Almost never."

"Not even when you were little?"

"My father broke it. He broke everything."

She lets him negotiate a corner. He's such a careful driver, there's something venerable about it. He might be asked to stand up someday at a luncheon: The Man Who Never Got a Ticket.

Then she tries again. "When you were a kid, what'd you want to be when you grew up?"

He doesn't take his eyes off the empty street. "Just, you know—alive. Look, is it okay if we make a stop? Somebody called in today about a beagle we adopted out last week."

Danny drives, encased in an aura of intent as securely as any debilitated boy in a bubble. Margaux likes being along for the ride, deciphering the simple code of his silence. And thinking about next year. Being away from home. Being paid to read.

Or rewarded, anyway. *Scholarship*. What a gorgeous word.

The houses turn run-of-the-mill, most of them pushed right against the street like people waiting for the doors to open at a big sale. There is a nimble-looking bike here and there belonging, no doubt, to a boy not old enough to drive yet mad for speed. But the cars are vanquished-looking, usually parked in front of garages bulging like predators' nests.

"Here we are."

A duplex is set back from the street. It cowers under a thick oak whose trunk leans like it has been in a high wind for a hundred years.

"This should be a piece of cake. Nobody's home."

"Where's the pooch?" Margaux asks.

Danny opens his door. "Out back, probably. Want to come?"

"I'm okay. Don't worry about me. I'll listen to the radio."

Almost before she can finish, he's past the sidewalk and through the dilapidated gate. Margaux takes a deep breath. Tonight she's just a pretty girl—wait! She's just a girl on a date. Meeting the boy's difficult aunt. Getting along, anyway. Having dinner. Finding things she and Danny have in common (reading, for example), just like *Seventeen* says. No big deal. Normalsville. Everyday City.

Except the next time she sees Danny, he's storming through the shadows, white moths rising from the tall grass at his feet.

He strides right past the window on her side, pounds on the trunk with his fist. "Son of a bitch."

She's stunned to hear him swear, more stunned when he returns seconds later with a baseball bat.

"What—"

He doesn't let her finish, probably wouldn't answer, anyway.

There's a car at the end of the driveway, sleek and, because of some errant sprinklers, damp as a merman. Danny walks right up to the grille, puts one foot on the generous bumper, takes a batter's stance, and then lets go.

He spares nothing—not a headlight or window. Not a door or side panel. And his blows are big: roundhouse, go-for-the-fences ones and huge executioner's strokes. In the streetlight's glare, his bat might be a flaming sword.

"Oh!"

She can't help it. The word flies out of her—part groan, part whimper. And louder, more clamorous than she planned if she had, in fact, planned. Which she didn't.

Shrapnel hits the windshield, hers, the one she's staring through. She winces, retreats, leans forward, fascinated and appalled. He's in a frenzy, a punishing dervish.

Margaux senses rather than sees the porch light go on across the street. When she does turn, there's that one and another. And a man in ghostly underwear standing in a door.

"Danny! Stop it. Get back in the car."

Does he hear her? He returns, but probably just because he's finished. He moves deliberately. More than that, actually. He swaggers.

The bat goes into the back; he slides into the front. Doesn't meet her eyes.

"Danny, what in the—"

With only a glance in the rearview mirror, he backs up so viciously the muffler scrapes and throws sparks. "Bruno didn't have any water."

"But," she begins, "that's no reason to—"

"And they had him on such a short leash, he was lying in his own poop." He revs the engine, drops the gear shift into drive, and patches out. In what light there is, his face has planes and angles she's never seen before.

"Danny, what's going—"

"Shut up." He turns to her, letting the car hurtle down the street on its own. He lifts one threatening finger.

Things fragment. She sees how sharp his nose is, how his left ear is bent in on itself. One eye is closed. Not in some grotesque parody of a wink, but as if it's swollen. Like after a fight.

"One more word," he says, "and you're next."

They plummet toward home. Her home. With her mom inside, just beyond the long dark lawn and the half-drowned, melancholy California poppies.

Once there, he just grips the wheel and stares

straight ahead. She fumbles for her door. Then exits. Decamps. Yet watches the taillights recede—they resemble the red glowing ends of cigarettes, the kind lovers used to light when they were spent.

A few days later, Sara stalks up to Margaux in the cafeteria.

"Are you going to sit by yourself forever?"

"I wouldn't be very good company."

"What's going on, anyway?"

"Danny and I broke up."

"About time. Why?"

"He just hasn't called me."

"You are like a million times better than him." She reaches for Margaux. "Come sit with us."

She lets herself be drawn to her feet but says, "I don't know if this is a good idea."

"Oh, c'mon. It'll be like old times."

She's led to Sara's table. Sara the cynosure. Sara who tells the girl at the end of the table, "Move your fat ass." So Margaux can take her old place as viceroy.

It starts immediately: "Did anybody watch the

Homework Channel last night? I love that black guy who teaches math."

"You mean algebra."

"Whatever. He's got dreads like down to his shoulders. He makes me want to add stuff up."

Another one prattles about the future, by which she means robot housekeepers and ozone cars that know the way home when you're too stoned to fly.

Sara fills Margaux in. "We were talking about this party at Marc's house Saturday. His parents are going out of town. He's already got two kegs."

"I want to know who's coming so I can not come if they are."

This pathetic excuse for a sentence arrives courtesy of a girl Margaux barely recognizes. Maybe doesn't recognize. Her hair is purple-black like a crow's wing. And she's a little hard to understand because the stud in her tongue looks big as a marble: "I ont due doe whooze gummy tho ah gan nod gum iv day ah."

Sara glances at Margaux, grins, rolls her eyes,

meaning, *This is what I had to put up with while you were gone.*

"Well, I don't want to see that bitch Jennifer."

"And not Gloria Albright. Her mother makes her clothes."

"Or her father, he is so gay."

"He *is* so gay. Did you see him in those pants!"

"Well, he came on to me."

"Oh, my God. You're kidding."

"No, he is such a creep."

"Was he at Max's party last year? Somebody felt me up while I was passed out."

"Like you'd know that."

Margaux looks around the table; this is not working. All of a sudden she's thinking about a safe room, something she's only heard of but suddenly wants: water, oxygen, bulletproof door, dead bolts, a thousand books. Utterly quiet. Completely silent. No girls she barely knows in saggy leather pants, no girls in mesh strippers' gloves and jeans sanded thin as a bee's wing, and no girls who can't stay home one night a year because they are always and forever out. On their way to. Coming from.

And then her heart opens. Just a little, but it does. Because she remembers all that. How she felt then: the self-reproach, the utter confusion. The relief of getting in somebody's car and going anywhere that wasn't her ugly living room with her dazed mother and awful father, *awful* as in creepy, and *awful* as in huge/powerful/capable of inspiring awe. Anywhere away from that father and all the other fathers who couldn't keep their eyes or innuendoes off their daughters or their daughters' yummy friends.

That's why her heart opens. For those girls at the table who always feel baffled and sad, tender and malign, repulsive and desirable, innocent and contemptuous of innocence.

So she cries. For them, mostly. For herself a little. The other girls try to ignore it; maybe it'll stop and she'll go away. But Margaux doesn't stop. She cries louder, in fact. Kids nearby stop talking. Those across the room stand up. The servers in their hair-nets pause; in fact, everything hesitates. So that for a second there's no sound in the enormous room but that of Margaux sobbing.

There's a big fire somewhere east, near San Dimas. A pall hangs over the San Gabriel Valley. At stoplights, ash falls onto cars. The sun is just a doubloon. There are sirens everywhere.

Just past the racetrack's admission gates, bettors cluster under the TVs. Their eyes roll up like extras auditioning for the role of adoring Magi. Margaux makes her way among them effortlessly, relentlessly. Out here in the cheap seats, it's retirees mostly. Widowers. Pensioners. Men whose ancient wives are only too glad to see them leave the house. Men with no wives. Ever.

She knows her father's table in the Club House. And sure enough, there's Mom with her bodice-ripper paperback. There's Dad with his fifty-dollar haircut, silk shirt, and Bruno Magli shoes — a panther in the boneyard. She watches men sidle up to him. They're sheepish, almost bashful. Above all, they're deferential. When she arrives, he waves them away.

"What are you doing here, kiddo? Is everything okay? How did you find us?"

"When you weren't at home, where else would you be?"

"Why aren't you in school?"

"A little late to play the concerned parent, don't you think?"

He scowls. "What's got into you?"

Margaux takes a deep breath. "When I was ten, you'd tell Mom we were going to the movies. Then you'd drive me over to Tony's house and let him take pictures of me in my underpants."

He's on his feet. He's hissing. "What? Are you crazy?"

She stands her ground. He *is* handsome. If she got her beauty from him, does that mean . . .

"I asked if you were crazy."

She leans in, gets a whiff of his cologne, which smells like a forest with a urinal. "How could you do that? How could you let Tony do that?"

"Will you sit down and shut up, or do you want me to have you thrown out of here? Is that what you want? Because I can do it."

She lowers herself into a chair. Likes the feel of the decorative metal against her back. "Aren't you ashamed?"

Her mother puts her fork down. "Margaux, are you on drugs? You have seemed unfocused lately. You've been neglecting your homework, and I'm not sure I approve of some of your new friends. Those are all signs of— "

"I was ten years old. My underpants had kittens on them."

Her mother hisses across her chef's salad. "Tony wouldn't do anything like that. He's a Catholic."

"Dad? You've got to talk to me. Either talk to me or I start screaming. I'll tell everybody."

"I was paying off a debt, okay? A big one. I explained all that. On the way over there."

"Then you just kept borrowing, didn't you? Because you took me back a lot. I was like money in the bank."

"Did he ever lay a hand on you? No. I made sure of that. Anyway, it was like a bathing suit, what you had on. Half a bikini. That's all they wear in Europe."

"I hate you, do you know that? I hate you. You're a disgrace."

Now her mother stands. A napkin falls from her lap like a doomed parachutist. "Margaux. Shut your mouth, and I mean now. Who do you think you are?"

Her father sighs. "Fine, you hate me. But it was either let Tony take the pictures or they were going to hurt me. You know Tony. The kind of person he is. Who he works for. Those wise guys don't kid around."

"You're not even sorry."

"I am, I am too. You think I'm proud of myself for that? I didn't sleep too good afterward, okay?"

"Say 'I'm sorry.'"

"Sure, I am. Who wouldn't be." He picks up part of a roll and butters it. He's very good with the knife. Very deft. He can't help himself; he glances at the TV, at the fifth race from Belmont. That's how important this is to him.

She stands, looks at her mother, whose jaw is quivering but who now pretends to be buried in her lurid novel. "I never," Margaux says, struggling to keep her voice steady, "need to see either one of you again for as long as I live." She puts the keys to the Mustang beside the salt and pepper shakers. "You're toxic, both of you. And I don't want anything you ever gave me."

She turns and strides away. Both knees are weak, but she wills that not to matter. She ducks into the first women's restroom, leans into the nearest sink, runs cold water, and plunges her face into it. She stays under for a while, relishing the shock, the eerie hush. Then she surfaces and stands there, water trickling down her face and neck, into her blouse. She's almost as wet as Venus. And just as reborn.

Outside, the fire might be under control. The air doesn't have that tang of disaster. Things have stopped falling from the sky. Chicken Little can relax.

Only once on the way out does she stop and sob. Women — always women — appear beside her. "Honey, are you all right? Do you need a ride home? Do you need some money?"

She shakes her head, but lets them put an arm

around her shoulders, walks with them to the line of taxis, where drivers stand around under the palm trees lying about blondes.

She gets into the first one and gives him the address.

At Danny's house, she pays the cabdriver, then stands on the sidewalk. She starts up the walk, changes her mind, starts again. Finally she climbs the five steps and knocks. Retreats a little.

He answers the door, turning sideways and peering out.

"Can I see Evie? Just for a minute."

Danny glances over one shoulder. "She's not doing too well today."

He has a shirt on, a new one.

"You look nice."

"For a change?"

"No. It fits and everything."

"I went shopping." He points. "In Arcadia. At the mall. That was weird."

"Isn't it? I used to like it, but . . . I don't know. You're right. It's just weird." Margaux shivers and tugs at the lapels of her short leather jacket. "How's—"

"Bruno?"

"Yeah."

"He's okay. Luc went over and got him. And if you're wondering about that car, Evie sent a money order kind of anonymously, so I owe her something like ten million dollars." He slumps against the door. "That was—that thing that happened on the way home from there—that was my old man talking."

"You scared me."

"Tell me about it. I scared myself!"

Evie appears. "Who are you talking to, Danny?"

"Just me." Margaux embraces Evelyn, who is hot and smells sharply acidic.

"Do you want to come in, honey? It's cold out here."

"No, that's all right. This won't take long; I just want to brag a little. I finally rebuked my parents, and I'm kind of proud of myself."

"You did what?" Evie's eyes look flat and varnished.

Margaux leans closer. "Like the Torah said, remember? Don't just hate somebody in your heart; rebuke him."

"What are you talking about? I'm not Jewish." Evelyn turns to her nephew. "Do you know what she's talking about?"

Now Danny steps back; now he lets the door swing open. "Maybe," he says, "you'd better come in."

EPILOGUE

They're drying dishes. She's drying, actually. Danny's washing, and he's wearing blue rubber gloves. Plus an apron with a rooster on it. He stacks things on a wooden rack. She dries and puts them away. A plate and a cup. A pot and a pan.

Danny runs cold water, chases the suds toward the drain. Off come the gloves. He slaps them down on the counter like a swordsman about to challenge someone to a duel.

Instead he takes off the apron and hangs it on a hook. More than a hook, actually. A brass index finger crooked invitingly. Then he smoothes his sweater with both hands.

"This is the nicest thing I ever owned. Is it really cashmere?"

"Yes, but no cashmeres were injured during the weaving of that sweater."

"Isn't this stuff expensive?"

"It was on sale. And I got my employee discount."

Danny pets his sleeve. "I love this thing."

"I was afraid you wouldn't take it; I wanted to throw it on the sidewalk and let you find it, but Evie made me leave it in its box."

"Did you see Sara's Christmas present in the parking lot at school?"

"Her parents are really something. They sleep on satin pillowcases."

"Why satin?"

"So when they wake up, their faces aren't all creased."

"People are so weird. You gotta love 'em." He walks to the refrigerator, takes out a can of ginger ale, holds it up inquisitively.

"Half," says Margaux.

"Glass?"

She shakes her head, follows him to the table, sits. A wooden bowl near her elbow holds vegetables: a spaghetti squash, two burly onions, a big, loud red pepper.

He drinks from the can, holds it out to her. The metal is not so cold where his mouth was.

"My mother," she says, "thinks I'm in a cult."

"Wait'll the cops bust in and find us all reading." He tries for a tough-guy delivery. "It'll be curtains for sure."

"She says now that everything's out in the open, we can forgive and forget. Get on with our lives. Or at least that's what she thinks Dr. Phil would say."

"Did you see your dad this time?"

"He was playing cards. Mom says he can't lose lately. He hasn't been this hot in years. Go figure, huh?"

He takes her hand, holds it in both of his. And she knows that will be that. Every now and then she wishes he were good-looking, with strong tennis player's legs. Somebody who would make demands on her. Legitimate ones.

"Who reads," he asks, "to Evie tonight?"

"I do."

"You work late tomorrow, don't you? I should pick you up after. Stop and see a collie on the way home."

"How's Rex?"

"Back at the shelter. His owners returned him. I guess he didn't fit."

"Or was the wrong color."

In the distance, Margaux hears a train. The long warning whistle. People going somewhere.

She stands. "I'll get ready for bed and then read to Evie."

"I'll see you in the morning."

The bland embrace, the dry kiss on the cheek.

In the bath just off the bedroom that is officially hers, she brushes her teeth, then puts on a clean T-shirt and, because Evie likes the house cold, white leggings and socks.

Then she pads down the hall, past Danny's bedroom with its two enormous posters (one of the periodic table, the other of Sananda, who looks like Jesus but isn't). She knocks on Evie's door, goes in without waiting.

Evelyn is propped up on five or six pillows. She opens her eyes. "I wasn't asleep," she quips, "just resting everything from my forehead down."

"Do you need to go to the bathroom?"

"I'd better."

Margaux throws backs the covers.

"Let's try to walk tonight," Evie says. "That wheelchair depresses the crap out of me."

Margaux loops an arm around one shoulder, gets the other around Evie's waist, and they make their way across the cool floor.

"See those little cat prints?" Evie gestures toward her feet. "The tiles with those in them cost more, and I didn't care. I loved the idea of clay drying in the sun and some big old tom sauntering across them on his way to an assignation."

Margaux pushes the bathroom door open. Gets to the toilet. "I'm okay now," Evie says. "I can do the rest."

Margaux leaves her alone, fusses with the bedclothes a little, looks out the window toward the lawn and the street beyond. A car goes by blasting rap music, leaving a little bit of some corporate-sponsored ghetto in its wake.

"How was lunch with your mother?" Evelyn shouts.

Margaux crosses toward the bathroom. She speaks through the not-quite-closed door. "Weird."

"Do you pray for her?"

"Are you kidding? She's not gonna change."

"You wouldn't be praying for her to change. She'd just be in your prayers."

"I'm not like you guys."

"I know." No rancor, no disappointment. Said with perfect equanimity. Then, "You can come in now." Evie's standing, leaning on the sink. "That made me tired. Call Sir Hillary. Tell him to start the ascent of K2 without me."

On their way back to the bed, Margaux asks, "What should I read tonight?"

"The sleep poem. I love that. All that stuff in the first stanza actually happened to me, did I tell you?"

"Uh-uh."

"My parents went to big, noisy parties and took me. Just about the time people got really smashed, I'd go out like a light and somebody would carry me upstairs to . . . How does that line go?"

"To 'a dark lake of coats.'"

Evie slides out of Margaux's grasp, lets her legs be lifted onto the bed, lets herself be covered up. "God, I hate this."

"I'll be right back. Don't go anywhere."

"The old jokes are the best, aren't they?"

Margaux crosses the room, plucks the book off the shelf. It falls open on its own.

Evie pats the bed. "Sit here. Let me hold your hand."

They're like that. Both of them—hand holders. Maybe it runs in the family.

"Did I tell you I'm going blind in one eye?" Evie blurts. "Well, I am. Don't tell Danny. He'll just worry. But it complicates my prayers. If I say, 'Let me see,' she's liable to just give me insight. And I hate, 'Improve my vision.' I feel like I'm writing copy for an optometrist."

"So God's a girl now?"

"This week."

"Do you want some water?"

"Am I babbling?"

"Your lips look dry."

"No, no water. Just read the poem."

Margaux almost knows it by heart, but she opens the book anyway. She's barely through the second stanza before Evie is breathing evenly.

She slips out, closes the door behind her. She likes to walk through the house when everything's asleep. Not just the people but everything—timber and lath, foundation and pipes, water and gas, dish and spoon.

Margaux checks the heavy doors, returns a book to its place on the shelf, straightens a chair.

She's tempted to just stay here. Work at Macy's (where she's liked, where she already has return customers who rely on her good taste), drive Evie's Porsche sometimes, read after dinner, and watch the play of firelight on the cruets of oil and vinegar at the end of the oak table.

But she won't. It's too seductive, and she's had enough of that. In a way, she prefers the difficult hours—an injured dog, a feverish Evie. But even that has its own questionable magnetism: *What a good girl am I.*

No, she's heard from three schools already. She'll hear from more. And then she'll decide.